When the play was over, Leda asked if I wanted to come back to her house. She said it was right near the theater.

She had an interesting room. It was huge, much bigger than mine, with all kinds of posters on the wall. Some seemed to be from plays her mother might have been in. There was also a big subway map of New York and a photo of her in a long fancy dress.

"That was when I was in this school play," she said. "I think I look sort of sexy there, for me." She smiled at me. She was sitting down, leaning against her bed. "Are you almost blind without your glasses," she said, "or can you see a little bit?"

"I can see a little bit." I sat down next to her. I took my glasses off. "I can see you."

I leaned over and kissed her. Her lips were really soft.

"Do you like me?" she asked. "Do you want to go out again?"

Fawcett Books
by Norma Klein:

COMING TO LIFE
DOMESTIC ARRANGEMENTS
FRENCH POSTCARDS
IT'S OKAY IF YOU DON'T LOVE ME
LOVE & OTHER EUPHEMISMS
LOVE IS ONE OF THE CHOICES

NORMA KLEIN
Beginners' Love

FAWCETT JUNIPER • NEW YORK

RLI: $\dfrac{\text{VL: 5 + up}}{\text{IL: 10 + up}}$

A Fawcett Juniper Book
Published by Ballantine Books

Library of Congress Catalog Card Number: 82-18522

ISBN 0-449-70091-7

This edition published by arrangement with Hillside Books/E.P. Dutton,
Inc.

Manufactured in the United States of America

First Ballantine Books Edition: April 1984

For Richard Peck

1

My best friend, Berger, is in love with Brooke Shields's eyebrows. He says if he ever meets a girl with eyebrows like that, he's going to marry her or, anyway, fall madly in love with her. I tell you this just to explain what we were doing at a two o'clock showing of *Endless Love,* which got pretty rotten reviews from everyone. It's the kind of movie Berger's little sister, Hope, would go to see: she's eleven. It also happened to be the week before school started and there wasn't a whole lot to do.

Berger and I go to the same school, Willard. It used to be called The Willard School for Boys, but a couple of years ago the trustees voted to make it coed. The trouble is, the way they're doing it, they started at fifth grade, which is where the school begins, so now the only coed grades are up through sixth. Maybe when we're about thirty they'll have gotten around to having girls in the last year of high school, which is where we'll be this year. Some of the sixth grade girls aren't bad, but they aren't much older than Hope. You look more at them and realize that by the time you graduate college, some of them may be terrific.

Despite this, Berger manages to have what you could call a social life and I don't, proving that personality or something enters in, as well as opportunities or lack of them. If he were outstandingly handsome or a great athlete, I could use that as an excuse, but he's around ten pounds overweight and—well, not ugly, but no one ever suggested he enter a Robert Redford look-alike contest. The thing with Berger, as opposed to me—I'm not mentioning any of this to be self-deprecating, just to give you an accurate picture—is that he talks to girls wherever he happens to be, whether he knows them or not. Sometimes that can be embarrassing.

We were sitting there, waiting for the movie to begin, when Berger shoved me in the ribs. "One row up, four seats down," he said.

"What?"

"Hey, wait, they're moving down." He lowered his voice. "They're right in front of us."

All I could see was the back of two girls' heads. One was wearing a felt hat, and the other had long dark hair that hung over the back of her shirt. Berger grinned at me. I knew he was going to try something. He leaned forward and tapped the shoulder of the girl with the hat. "Uh, miss, do you think you could take your hat off during the show? My friend here has a seeing problem."

The girl with the hat turned around. She was blond and very pretty. "What kind of problem?" she said. "Where's his dog?"

"I didn't say he was blind," Berger said. "He just can't see through hats."

2

"Tough. . . . Move, then."

"A real sweetie," Berger said, loud enough for her to hear. "I guess she can't take her hat off because she's going bald at an early age. They say girls who're on the Pill start going bald really early."

There was a snort of laughter from one of the girls, it wasn't clear which. Then the girl in the hat said, "They say boys who're too ugly to pick up girls start getting softening of the brain in their teens. Some of them can't even get into colleges like the University of Southern Vermont."

"*Is* there a University of Southern Vermont?" the dark-haired girl said seriously.

The movie credits started going on.

"Uh, miss," Berger said. "If you're going to talk during the movie, I'll have to speak to the usher. It disturbs my concentration."

The girl in the hat didn't even turn around.

Berger sighed and smiled at me. I could tell he wasn't ready to give up yet.

The movie was bad. It wasn't unenjoyable, though. It was the kind of movie where you could follow what was going on, but still be thinking of another dozen things at the same time. Maybe because of that, I didn't notice when the sound track went dead. It was a scene where the hero is hiding outside his girl friend's house, watching a party she's at and getting jealous because he thinks she's making it with some other guy. Brooke Shields was standing there, kind of smiling at the other guy, when someone next to us yelled, "Sound!" Then Berger yelled, "Come *on,* you guys!" A woman got up and walked to the door. It was then that I realized there hadn't been any sound at all for about five minutes. I thought it was just because the hero wasn't at the party, that all the noise was inside his girl friend's home. We sat there for another five minutes with the movie going, but no sound. The hero went into a phone booth and started talking, but you couldn't hear anything.

"Oh, Christ," the girl in the hat said.

"I think someone went to tell them about it," her friend said.

About two minutes later the movie stopped altogether. They kept the theater lights off, though.

"What should we do?" the girl with the long hair said, in a worried voice. "Do you think they'll give us our money back?"

"They'll fix it," the girl in the hat said. "Don't worry." She took out some wool from a bag and started knitting.

"How can you do it in the dark?" her friend said.

"I know the pattern by heart," the girl in the hat said. She put her feet up on the seat in front of her. She was wearing jeans and sneakers.

All of a sudden Berger got to his feet.

"Where are you going?" I asked nervously.

"You'll see." He started down the aisle. When he came to the front of the theater, he jumped up on the stage. He made his hands into a megaphone. "Can everybody hear me?" he said.

"Oh no, *now* what?" said the girl in the hat wearily, stopping her knitting.

"I just want everyone to keep calm," Berger said. You could hear him down to the back row. "No need to panic. The show'll be on in a couple of minutes. We're having a few technical difficulties. Keep cool, folks. . . . I just have a few words from the management. Would anyone wearing a hat in the theater please remove it at once. It's not that we want to inhibit your movements. Just health regulations."

Can you believe this? I saw two people taking their hats off. Not the girl in front of us, though. She just said to her friend, "Who let *him* out?"

Someone from the audience yelled, "So, when's the show going to start?"

"I told you," Berger said. "Just be patient, okay? And while you're waiting, I'm going to act out some of your favorite scenes from the movie."

There was a whistle. "How about the sex scenes?" someone said.

"Why not?" Berger said, pretending to start taking his shirt off. "If you've got a great body, why not show it, as Miss Piggy says? . . . Now all I need is a little help from the audience. Is there a young lady out there who'd like to join me? Don't be bashful, girls. You don't have to look like Brooke Shields, though if you do, that's okay too. . . . Hey, Blondie, you with the knitting, can you act?"

"I don't *believe* this," the blonde said. She called out, "Shut up and get off the stage, will you, you jerk."

Berger stretched out his hands. "Okay, so I'll act the scenes by myself. It's more fun with a girl, but . . ." Just as he was about to do something, God knows what, the movie started again. I felt relieved. I was afraid they were going to kick both of us out of the theater. Berger jumped off the stage and came back down to our seats.

Berger wants to be an actor. At this camp where we were CITs this year, he always gets the leads. This summer he was Sherlock Holmes in *The Hound of the Baskervilles*. He has dark red hair, but they sprayed it black. He was really good. He had around a thousand lines and he didn't forget one of them. His father doesn't want him to be an actor, though. I guess he thinks it's not that reliable a profession, compared to a lawyer, which is what he is. I haven't decided yet about what I want to be. I used to think a doctor, but then you have to stay in school till you're around thirty. That's another thirteen years of my life. I don't think I could take that.

The rest of the movie was okay. It wasn't that sexy,

though. I read somewhere that it wasn't Brooke Shields's body. They used the body of some other girl. That doesn't seem fair. They didn't even give her a credit. If it's a singer and they dub it, they at least say that. Maybe the girl whose body it was would've been a better actress than Brooke Shields. If I were her, I'd be mad.

As we were walking out, Berger turned around and said to the two girls, who were coming up the aisle behind us, "So, how'd you like it?" He said it in this perfectly friendly way, like they were our dates or something. I thought for sure the blond one was going to say something really sarcastic, but she just said, "Boring."

"He's in love with Brooke Shields's eyebrows," I said, just to say something. I looked over at the girl with the long dark hair. She wasn't as pretty as the blond girl, but she had nice eyes.

"The rest of her isn't bad," Berger said.

"That wasn't the rest of her," I said. "It was somebody else's body."

"Huh," Berger said. "What d'you know? Whose body?"

"Mine," the blond one said and grinned. Actually, she was small and not that sexy-looking from the neck down.

"And they didn't even give you a credit," Berger said, shaking his head. "Terrible."

"My friends know," the blonde said. "They recognize my birthmark."

"Where is it?" Berger said.

The blonde was still smiling. "Didn't you notice it?"

"Why don't you show us?"

"Not on a first date."

A first date! Okay, so it looked like we had picked them up. Or maybe they had picked *us* up. Anyhow, whatever was going on seemed to be mainly going on between Berger and the blond girl. We went to a coffee shop with them.

Berger and I sat on one side of the booth and the two girls sat on the other.

"I'm Leda and this is Danielle," the blonde said.

"You like swans, huh?" Berger said.

"Used to," said Leda, "but you just can't trust them. . . . So, did you like it or didn't you?"

"It wasn't that great," I said.

"What gets me," Leda said vehemently, "is she can't even act! They ought to pass some law saying models aren't allowed to even *try* to act. They just kind of stand there. What connection is there between looks and acting, anyway? Do you go up to a pretty girl on the street and say, 'I'd like to take you home and have you write a novel for me'?"

Berger grinned. "You could try. . . . Give her typing paper, anyway."

There was a slight pause.

"I thought the book was better," the dark-haired girl, Danielle, said. She seemed sort of shy. She'd look up and then look down right away.

Leda pointed to her. "She reads *everything*. . . . You name it. . . . She's read it."

"The book was just completely different," Danielle said. She seemed to be looking mostly at me, but maybe that was just my imagination.

"What was different about it?" I asked.

"Well, like, the boy's father had a Black girl friend and they left that out. . . . And the heroine had an affair with another girl."

"Brookie with another girl?" Berger said. "Never."

"Why never?" snapped Leda.

"What does she need with a girl?" Berger said.

"Maybe she thinks boys are dumb," Leda said. "Ever think of that?"

"No one with eyebrows like that could think boys are dumb," Berger said.

7

Leda had a round face and freckles. She definitely wasn't going bald. Her hair was blond and curly and she had two feather earrings hanging from her ears. On her shirt she had two buttons: "He's cute, but can he type?" and "Castrate rapists." Danielle had a thinner face. Her nose was a little too long, but she was pretty anyway.

"I got really scared when you jumped up on the stage," Danielle said to Berger. "I thought maybe you were one of those guys that goes berserk and shoots ten people."

"Never . . . I'm harmless."

"They could've kicked you out," Leda said thoughtfully, spooning up some whipped cream off her hot chocolate. It was eighty-seven degrees out, but she'd ordered hot chocolate. The rest of us had Cokes. "You do that kind of thing a lot?"

When we got out of the coffee shop, Berger said, "Want to share a cab?"

"We have our bikes," Danielle said, pointing to where they were chained up against a lamp post.

"Okay, well, give us your numbers in case we have a free evening some time."

Leda gave him a dirty look. "555–8562. . . . What's yours?"

"555–4332."

I know I should have said something to Danielle, asked for her number, but I didn't. We started walking off. The second we were out of sight, Berger got out a pencil and wrote Leda's number on a piece of paper.

I sighed. "I should've asked for the other girl's."

"No sweat. . . . I'll get it for you."

"What if she gave you the wrong number?"

"Not a chance." He smiled. "She was cute. I like the feisty type."

One major difference between Berger and me in relation

8

to girls is this: He always thinks about whether *he* likes *them.* I always think about whether *they* like *me.*

"What did you think of the dark-haired one?" I said. We decided to walk home. Berger lives about ten blocks from me, on Central Park West and Eighty-fourth Street. I live on Seventy-fourth.

"Great figure . . . Kind of quiet."

I hadn't even noticed her figure! "How could you tell?"

"What?"

"About her figure."

"What do you mean, how could I tell?"

"Well, she had that loose shirt on."

Maybe it's because he has a sister that Berger is more observant about girls than I am, and more relaxed with them. I just have a brother—Knox. He's fifteen years older than me and is an oral surgeon, which is a fancy kind of dentist. Mom and Dad worry because he's over thirty and not married yet. He lives in L.A. and only dates really gorgeous girls. Dad says if they have a scratch on them, he tosses them back. Last time he was visiting us, Dad said to him, "Knox, if you go on like this, you're going to end up a very lonely, envied old man."

"So, you're really going to ask her out?" I pursued. Berger jokes around so much, it's hard to tell sometimes.

"Sure, why not?"

"She didn't seem to like boys that much."

He wrinkled his nose. "That's just an act. . . . She probably goes down like a wounded water buffalo."

Despite all his talk, Berger has actually only made it in the total sense with one girl. She was the drama counselor at our camp, Marilyn Globerman. She was a couple of years older than we were, a sophomore in college, and she directed the play when the guy they'd hired to direct couldn't do it because his mother was sick. She thought Berger was really talented, but she wouldn't do much with

9

him while camp was on because it's against the rules. If the head of the camp sees you holding hands with a girl, he goes up to you with a kind of sickly smile and says, "It's not that kind of camp." Maybe he thinks everyone would be off making it in the woods every chance they got if he didn't say that. People that age forget it's not that easy to find anyone to do it with, someone who's moderate looking and not a total jerk. But when they got back to the city, Marilyn invited Berger over to her parents' apartment and they did it right away. He didn't have to talk her into it or anything. Berger says with college girls it's completely different. They don't have any hang-ups about wanting you to think they're virgins, according to him.

"What do you think about the other one?" I said.

"In what way?"

"Like what you just said."

"Does she put out?" He shrugged. "Maybe for someone ultra sensitive like you . . . if you fell on the floor in a writhing heap and promised to marry her and swore undying love. But short of that, I wouldn't count on it."

You may be getting the wrong idea. I don't have any hell-bent desire to get laid before college. I admit if the opportunity arose, I wouldn't run in the opposite direction, but the few girls that've liked me at all never seem to be the type. Berger says if you find the right buttons to push, they all are. So maybe I don't push the right buttons. Plus, I would kind of like her to be a reasonable human being, not a complete fool. I hope that doesn't rule out too many people.

❧ 2 ❧

My father is a restaurant critic. He didn't always used to be. He started out as a certified public accountant, the kind of guy that does people's taxes for them. I suppose that's a pretty steady job since people always have to pay taxes and most people can't figure out how to do it themselves. But he always liked to eat gourmet food and he and my mother ate out a lot. Quite often they'd take me, even when I was a little kid. I didn't always appreciate what we were having, but it was kind of interesting going to all these different places and trying all sorts of peculiar foods that most people don't even know exist.

What happened was that, just for fun, my father started reviewing restaurants for a small West Side paper started by some guy he knew. He was going to those places anyway—whenever a new restaurant opens in our neighborhood he checks it out right away—so I guess he figured if he could get paid just to write it up, why not? Eventually the paper folded, but someone connected with a gourmet food magazine had read his stuff and liked it and offered him a full-time job. I was just ten then and it must have seemed like a pretty chancy thing to do. But Dad was forty-seven and he says that's an age when most people start wishing they'd done something else for a living. Like his friend Max, who's a psychiatrist but decided he'd rather write musical comedies. Or this friend of Mom's, Lilly, who was in law school but dropped out to run her own catering service. I can understand that from having been in school for fourteen straight years. I'd kind of like to take next year off and just do nothing, but I'm not sure my parents will think that's such a great idea.

"My son will have the filet of smoked trout with horseradish sauce and I'll have the artichoke vinaigrette," Dad said. We were eating alone because Mom had a meeting to go to; she runs an art gallery in SoHo.

One thing Dad always does is order stuff for me that I don't necessarily want to eat. He says he has to try as many things a restaurant offers as possible to make sure they're good at everything. Also, he usually goes back to a place two or three times to see if they're consistent. If I ever make a face when he's ordering something for me, he'll say, "It's important to expand your taste horizons, Joel."

"Sure, Dad," I say. Why fight it?

You'd think my Dad would be fat, spending so much of his life eating or thinking about food, but he isn't. He's one of these naturally skinny people like me, which drive Mom crazy. She's not exactly plump, but she's always trying to lose five pounds.

The trout was okay, maybe a little salty; I shoved the horseradish sauce to one side. "Dad, you know, I was thinking, like, about next year?"

Dad had that kind of dreamy, intense expression he gets when he's trying to decide if something he's eating is good or not. "Which college to go to?" he said.

I cleared my throat. "Well, you know, how you switched from being an accountant to being a food critic because you got sick of doing the same thing day in, day out?"

"Well, it wasn't just a matter of being sick of it, but anyway—go on."

I took a deep breath. "I don't know if I want to go to college next year." Before he could freak out, I went on, "I want to go eventually. I just think I'm ready for a change."

"College *is* a change," Dad said. He switched plates with me so he could try the trout. "You don't have to go somewhere in New York. You could go to California, Colorado, anywhere."

I know basically Dad would like me to go where he went, Yale, but he thinks that by never mentioning it, he's using some kind of subtle psychology on me. Like he deliberately didn't say New Haven, even though that was probably what he was thinking. "It's not the place so much," I tried to explain. "It's more—well, didn't you ever get sick of just studying? I've been going to school since I was three!"

"Sure, I got sick of it," Dad said. "Everything is boring to some extent. But if you become one of those people who throws in the towel the second you're bored, you'll never do a damn thing with your life."

"I'm *not* that kind of person!" Sometimes my father gets me really mad, even though he's basically a good guy and reasonably understanding. "I'm just talking about one *year,* not the rest of my life."

The waiter was hovering near us, getting ready to clear away our dishes. "How did you like the trout, sir?" he asked my father. Usually people don't recognize my father. He writes his column under a pseudonym, Alphonse Daudet, some French writer he used to like in college.

13

"I think we found it a little on the salty side . . . What did you think, Joel?"

"Yeah. . . . It was okay." I guess I'd been more concentrating on our conversation.

The waiter poured more wine in Dad's glass and went away. Dad always lets me have wine when we go out. I have a little, but so far I don't that much get the point of it. It seems to me if you want to get drunk, hard liquor is better. Dad says it's not to get drunk but to enhance the meal or something.

"Okay," Dad said. "So let's just say, for the sake of argument, that you apply to various colleges, get in, and then ask for a year off. . . . What would you do with that year?"

You'll notice he was sneaking in my getting into a college, like he was afraid that maybe I'd never come back once I quit. "I thought maybe I'd just . . . Well, I'd like to go to Europe," I said, not looking at him, "just travel around."

"And where would the funds for this expedition come from?" He had this somewhat ironic expression that he gets fairly often.

"Well, Berger's uncle lives in Paris and he belongs to this rock group over there, and he thought maybe they could kind of introduce me to people and maybe I could earn some money playing guitar. That's how *he* started."

"And if that didn't pan out?"

"Something else might."

Dad just looked at me. "Sure, and something else might not. It just doesn't sound very thought out, Joel. I mean, if you wanted to study in Paris for a year, I could see that, if you thought your French was good enough, but just wandering around, hoping someone will hire you . . ."

My father *always* does that! It drive me crazy. I mean, obviously you can look at anything from two points of view.

So instead of thinking how great it is that I have an actual plan, he makes it sound like that's just an excuse, like I'm going to bum around and sleep all day. "Dad, I just told you—the whole *point* of this is I'm sick of studying. What's the point of going to Paris and studying *there?* It's just the same thing only in a different place."

"It isn't," Dad said irritably. "It's a whole new culture, a new language. You'd be imbibing new things every day. God, when I was your age I would have cut off my right *arm* for a chance to spend a year in Paris."

"I'd like to spend a year in Paris," I said, sighing. "It's not that."

Berger is always amazed that I spend so much time trying to explain things to my father. His feeling is that his father is a total jerk and why bother, that their generation is so totally different in every way, you might as well be talking to a wall. I don't always feel that way with mine, but this time I sort of did.

So for the rest of the meal I just dropped the subject. Sometimes Dad needs time to get used to certain ideas. Eventually he may come around. Not always, but sometimes.

School started. Nothing special. I'm taking Computer One and Calculus. The only good teacher is Mr. Quinlan, who teaches Experimental Math. Also, this year we got a real French person to teach us French. The woman who used to teach it was from Louisiana and she had such a heavy southern accent, it was like she was speaking some made-up language. French and Math are my favorite subjects. Occasionally I've liked English, depending on who's teaching it and what they give us to read. The one thing I almost always hate is Science, which is too bad if I want to be a doctor. They always make it so dull, at least to me.

"Did you call those girls we picked up yet?" I asked Berger after school, as we were waiting for the bus.

"Not yet. That's an idea, though. Maybe I'll try Blondie tonight. Should I get the other one's number for you?"

"Yeah, sure."

That night I was lying around, not doing anything special, when my father knocked on my door. "It's for you, Joel," he said. Then he kind of smiled. "I *think* it's a girl."

I hate it when my father does that. Obviously he must know it's a girl, if it is. I went into the kitchen since there's an extension in there and my parents were in the living room. "Hello?" I said.

"Oh, hi. Joel?" I didn't recognize the voice.

"Yeah?" I said, slightly cautiously.

"Um, it's me, Leda. . . . We were the ones who sat in front of you, at the movie."

"Oh, yeah, right." I was getting slightly confused. I thought Leda was the blond one.

"Well, the reason I'm calling is—I wondered if you might want to go to a play with me this Saturday, *Salome?* It's by Oscar Wilde. . . . See, my father runs this theater in the Village. You might have heard of it—Square One? So I, like, have these free tickets and I just thought . . . well, if you weren't doing anything."

"The four of us, you mean?" I stammered.

"No, I just thought maybe we could go. Unless you don't like plays or something. Or you're busy. . . . Or whatever."

I was silent a moment. By now I knew it was the blond girl on the phone. "Um, I'm Joel," I said.

She laughed. "I know!"

"No, the thing is, I just thought maybe . . . I wasn't the one who got up on stage. That's Berger, my friend."

"I know," she said. "That's how I got your number. I called him."

16

"Oh." I was still sort of confused.

"Listen, you don't have to go, it's okay. You thought I was Danny, right? You want to go out with her?"

"No," I said. "I just . . ." I took a deep breath and started again. "I'd like to go," I said.

"Great!" She sounded really pleased. "Well, listen, could you meet me at the theater maybe fifteen minutes before it starts? I've seen it already. It's really good."

After I hung up the phone, I still felt somewhat confused. First of all, girls don't tend to call me that often. They did for my brother. Even when he's home for a week, the phone rings for him about every other second. But the main thing was, I couldn't figure out what'd happened with Berger and Leda. Maybe he decided he liked Danny, the dark-haired one, better because she had bigger breasts or something. I decided to call him just to straighten it out.

"Look, she likes you, I guess," he said. "That's the way it goes."

"Did you call her like you said?"

"No, I was going to, but she called me, asking for your number."

"Huh."

"So, what's the problem?"

"No, it's not a problem exactly. . . . I just thought she liked *you.*"

"You can never tell with girls. She kept staring at you when we were in that coffee shop. I guess I'm not her type or something. Maybe I came on too strong."

"She wants me to go to a play with her."

"So, go!"

"I'm going to, but . . . Are you mad?"

"No! Listen, there are plenty more where she came from. Go to it."

"Are you going to ask her friend out?"

"Maybe. . . . She was kind of quiet."

"Yeah."

"That's not always a bad thing. . . . I'll see. So listen, have fun Saturday, okay?"

"I'll try."

Berger picks up girls pretty easily so I don't feel all that guilty about this, more just surprised. When I went back in my room, I kept thinking back on our being in the coffee shop. I didn't remember her looking at me especially. Maybe I just didn't notice. I mean, she'd look at me when she talked, but not in any special way that I could tell. Here's what I look like, just to give you an idea. I mean, obviously no one can really be objective about what they look like, but the bare facts are that I'm five nine, more skinny than fat. I have light brown hair, which my father would like me to cut more often, glasses that I've worn since fourth grade, brown eyes. I'm not bad-looking, but I'm sort of awkward with girls. I can't think of what to say to them! Berger says just go ahead and say anything. I realize that's probably a good idea, but I still can't do it.

I'm surprised Leda called me because she seemed so outgoing and self-confident. Maybe that's just a pose, I don't know. Also, she was really pretty, which makes me nervous. Berger would say it shouldn't, but you figure pretty girls have dozens of guys after them and can afford to be really choosy about who they go out with. So if you don't measure up, they probably figure why bother. Maybe because I didn't say much, she figured I was really smart, but once she's out with me alone, she'll change her mind.

I'm doing what I shouldn't do, worrying about it ahead of time. Mom says the things you worry about rarely happen. The bad things that do happen are the things you never bothered to worry about because they're so unlikely or rare that you wouldn't even have thought of them. When I was in bed, trying to go to sleep, I thought of how she'd said it was her body in the movie. She was just joking, of course.

18

You could tell that because the girl in the movie was really tall, the girl whose body they used, and Leda was really short, maybe just five feet or so. Still, while I was jerking off, I kept imagining various scenes from the movie with that girl's body and Leda's face.

I hope I don't think about sex a lot when I'm on the date with her. She might be able to tell.

❧ 3 ❧

Berger's little sister, Hope, is really cute. Don't start thinking I'm a pervert or anything. I realize she's only eleven. Maybe that's why she's so cute and when she's fourteen or sixteen and a real knockout, like I'm sure she's going to be, she'll be all self-conscious about her looks. Right now she doesn't even have that much of a figure. She has really tiny breasts that you don't even notice unless she's wearing a leotard, which she often does because she's a gymnastics whiz. She can do splits and stand on her head. The kid has a lot of energy, totally unlike Berger.

Before we went to camp this summer, Berger's father took me aside and said he'd pay me five dollars for every tennis match I could play with Berger. He wanted him to get some exercise. I said I didn't feel I could accept the money, plus I knew it wouldn't work. What Berger likes about the camp is that nothing is compulsory and sports are definitely not a big deal. They're there, but most kids are more into music or acting or photography. I think I got Berger out on the court once all summer. He's not such a bad player—he just won't run for the ball. If it's more than two feet in front of him, he just looks at it and shrugs.

"I have a permit," Hope said, showing me. I dropped over there Saturday morning, the day of my famous date, to check Berger's history notes.

"Terrific," I said.

"Would you play with me sometime, Joel?" Hope said. "I'm good. I can get it over the net."

"Sure," I said.

"When?"

"I don't know."

"Tomorrow?" she said excitedly. "Could you do it tomorrow?"

"Yeah, that'd be okay."

She was standing on her head on the couch. "I have this great idea," she said, in the same excited voice. "You could be my coach. I could get really good, like Tracy Austin. I'm not going to stay this small all my life, you know. I bet this year I might grow six inches. That's what Berger did. He grew six inches in one year."

Hope really idolizes Berger. It's not fair. Or anyway, it's not logical. It's not based on his having such a wonderful character or anything. I guess it's just because he's her brother. Like, sometimes when she kids around, she calls him Berger King and for his birthday she made him this real gold crown with jewels all over it. Whenever she quotes something he said or did, it's like it's the word of God. I wish I had someone in my family who thought that way about me. My mother is basically on my side in most things, but when it comes to big issues, like this thing of my taking a year off before college, she tends to close ranks with my father. I don't think you could say she idolizes me in any case.

"I don't know how good I'd be as a coach," I said. It was a little hard talking to her while she was upside down. "I think maybe for that you should take lessons with a real pro."

Hope flipped over and sat cross-legged on the couch. "I did!" she said. "I took six lessons. I know how to do a two-handed backhand. I know how to do everything. I just need practice."

"Well, maybe the thing is to find someone your own age and go out and play with them a lot. That's the best way to learn."

She looked hurt. "So, you don't want to play with me because I'm too young?"

"No. . . . Listen, I *do* want to play with you. I just don't think I'd be a good coach. I can play, but I don't do everything the right way."

"I think you do," she said seriously. "I watched you once. . . . What don't you do the right way?"

"Well, like my serve . . . I don't toss it high enough. I make a lot of double faults."

"Oh." She just sat there staring at me. Hope has beautiful big blue eyes. I guess it's that little kids like that have a way of just staring at you. They don't try to hide what they feel—they don't even know about that. I wonder how long that'll last with her. Maybe another year at most. "So, who's this girl you're going out with?" she said.

I laughed nervously. "What girl?"

"I thought you were going out with some girl. . . . That's what Berger said. He said she was really pretty."

"Yeah, well, it's tonight. We're going to a play. Her father owns a theater."

"Is she?"

"What?" One bad habit I have is I don't always listen.

Like, right in the middle of a conversation I tune out, sometimes just for a few seconds, but then I realize I didn't hear what the person said. Berger calls it "being in orbit." "Have you come down from orbit yet, Joel?" he'll say.

"Is she *pretty?*" Hope said impatiently.

"Yeah," I said. "Pretty much."

Hope was silent a minute. "Do you think I'm going to be popular with boys?" she asked.

"Definitely," I said. I didn't want her to get conceited, but that's what I really think.

"They don't seem to like me now that much." She looked worried.

"Well, at your age, boys are sort of scared of girls," I explained.

"How come? What are they scared of?"

"I don't know. . . . They just are."

"When do they stop being scared?"

I thought. "I don't know. . . . I guess by the time they get married or something."

Hope sat staring at me. "That's a long time," she said finally.

Then I realized I was giving her the wrong impression. I remember how when I was Hope's age I went to this all-boys' camp that used to meet with the all-girls' camp across the lake and some guys eleven or twelve were going steady with girls. "Not everyone is scared," I amended. "Some guys are more . . . outgoing or whatever."

"Which kind are you?"

I swallowed. "I guess I'm in between," I said.

"I'm in between too," she said, and got up and walked out. Then a second later she came in again. "See you tomorrow, okay?"

That night my parents were going out to dinner. They left at six thirty. I was just lying around my room, listening to my

23

records. I have some terrific ones from the sixties that Knox gave me, some of the real guitar greats like Jeff Beck and Eric Clapton. Not that I ever expect to get that good, but you can learn a lot listening to them. My parents like me to keep my door closed when I do that because it's not the kind of music they like and they claim it's too loud. They should hear Berger. He turns his records on so loud the whole apartment rattles.

"We'll be back around midnight," Mom said, looking in. She looked around my room with that expression of wondering why it was so messy, but not wanting to get into it just before she went out. "Maybe you could go through that stuff in your closet," she said.

"Mom, the thing is, I'm going out," I said, "so I don't think I'll have time tonight."

"Tonight?"

"Yeah."

"Who with? You didn't say anything."

I cleared my throat. "With this girl," I said.

"What? Joel, turn down the music, will you? I can't hear what you're saying *or* what I'm saying."

I turned it down. "With this girl," I said again.

"What girl?" She looked suspicious, probably because I'd waited till the last minute to mention it.

"She's a friend of Berger's," I said. "Her father owns this theater and she thought I might want to see a play with her."

"What play?"

"*Salome.*"

My mother looked pleased. "I've heard that's a very good production. . . . Do you have enough money?"

"Sure, I'm okay, Mom." I smiled at her reassuringly.

My mother smiled back. "Is she nice, Joel?"

"Very." I figured that was easier than saying "I really don't know her that well" or "We picked her up at the

24

movies." My mother isn't rampantly nervous, but she has a few panic buttons that it's just as well to avoid if you can.

"Have fun!" she said, as they left.

"You too," I said.

Leda was waiting in front of the theater when I arrived. I got off at the right subway stop, but I walked two blocks in the wrong direction. She looked really pretty, though in a completely different way from that time at the movies. She had a purple shirt on with gold threads in it, sort of Indian looking, and purple jeans.

The play was interesting. Sometimes my mind would wander, but that really wasn't the fault of the play. I'd start thinking about Leda and why she'd invited me and what would happen after the play, whether we'd go somewhere and make out and if so where, and what it would be like. But I still managed to follow it pretty well.

At the intermission we went and got orange drinks.

"That's my mother," Leda said. "The slave woman."

"It is?" I don't know why I said that. There's no reason it shouldn't be her mother. I just didn't know her mother was an actress.

"Daddy doesn't do that often," Leda said, "because it seems like nepotism, you know? And Mommy doesn't like him to either because she can get parts on her own. It's harder, though, now that she's in her fifties. I mean, there just aren't that many good parts for women that age. . . . And like, she doesn't want to just play grandmothers! That's why they don't want me to be an actress. They say it's such an unstable life."

"That's what my parents say about being a musician," I said.

"Is that what *you* want to be?"

"Well, probably not. I don't think I'm that talented.

25

. . . But I wouldn't mind trying it for a few years just to make sure."

"My parents say they don't care what I do as long as I have a well-rounded education. Like, they wouldn't let me go to Performing Arts, even though I got in. I guess they're right . . . sort of. But the thing is, which is inconsistent, Mom still says if she had to do it over she'd be an actress, even knowing what she knows now. She says she'd just like me to avoid all that heartache, if possible. But maybe you can't! I mean, don't you think it's better to do something you really like than just have some dull job?"

"Definitely," I said. She'd been talking really fast and her cheeks were all pink. She looked really pretty.

"I had to promise them I wouldn't act in any school plays all year!" Leda said. "They want me to really buckle down till I get into college. But I still go to plays a lot." She looked up at me. "Did you wish it was Danny that'd called you up? Tell me truthfully."

"No," I said.

"Would you have called *me* up if I hadn't called you?"

"Sure," I lied. "I was planning to, but we get a lot of homework at this school I go to. And I didn't have your number."

"I gave it to you," she said, looking surprised.

"Well, I thought you were giving it to Berger."

She shook her head. "He's not my type. . . . He seems a little crazy. I mean, I'm sorry to say that if he's a good friend of yours."

"He's not actually crazy," I said. "He's more . . . He does impulsive things sometimes."

Leda looked at me. "Yeah, well, I do too . . . sometimes. So, you didn't mind that I called you?"

I shook my head.

"Some guys have these hang-ups about wanting to take

26

the initiative or whatever. But you didn't seem like that so much."

Actually, I'm not sure what type I am. "I think Berger liked your friend," I said. "We could go out together sometime maybe." I'm not sure why I said that. It's true Berger never said he didn't like her friend, but it was Leda he seemed to like better.

"The thing with Danny," Leda said, leaning close to me, "is that she's sort of shy. She isn't with me, at all. But with boys she tends to be. . . . And also, well, this is like a weird problem to have, but she has these very large breasts, and sometimes boys just go after her for that, really gross boys. . . . She might have this operation to have them made smaller when she's older." She laughed. "I guess she could give some to me."

"You seem fine to me," I said, looking down at her breasts. As soon as I said that, I turned red. It was a dumb thing to say, as though I'd been noticing her figure right from the start. I had been, but I was afraid she might classify me with those boys she doesn't like.

❧ 4 ❧

When the play was over, Leda asked if I wanted to come back to her house. She said it was right near the theater. "My parents usually go out after the play," she said. "But listen, I just want to warn you. If you're there when they come back, my father'll probably offer to drive you home. He doesn't think it's safe to wander around New York at night. . . . But you don't have to say yes, if you don't want."

"My parents are like that too," I said.

"It's partly because they're older," she explained. "Like, Danny's parents are just around forty. . . . But Mom wanted to really give her all to her career, so they didn't even have me till she was thirty-eight and he was forty. And, like, I'm their only child so they tend to be mildly obsessive about some things."

"My parents are old too," I said. It was interesting because I haven't met that many kids whose parents are. "They had my brother and then, for some reason, they waited fifteen years to have me."

"How come they waited so long?"

"I don't know."

"Maybe your mother had lots of miscarriages in between. My aunt was like that."

I shrugged. I just didn't know. They'd never explained it.

"So, it's almost like you're an only child, like me," Leda said. "Or are you real close to your brother?"

I shook my head. "Not at all."

"Sometimes I kind of wish I had a brother or sister to talk to," Leda said wistfully, "but basically I don't mind being an only child. You read all these articles about how people hate it, but I don't. . . . Maybe I'm sort of spoiled, though." She looked worried.

"You don't seem to be," I said, to reassure her.

"I like to have my own way," she admitted.

Leda had an interesting room. It was huge, much bigger than mine, with all kinds of posters on the wall. Some seemed to be from plays her mother might have been in. There was also a big subway map of New York and a photo of her in a long fancy dress.

"That was when I was in this school play," she said. "I think I look sort of sexy there, for me. They gave me this special kind of bra, that kind of, I don't know, whatever—" She smiled at me. She was sitting down, leaning against her bed. It was covered with blue corduroy. A small brown bear was tossed to one side. "Are you really, like, almost blind without your glasses," she said, "or can you see a little bit?"

"I can see a little bit," I said. I sat down next to her. I took my glasses off. She was about three inches away from me. "I can see you."

"I probably look better with your glasses off." She was staring at me, almost the way Hope does. She had really long eyelashes, darker than her hair.

I leaned over and kissed her. I had the feeling she expected me to. Also, I wanted to. Her lips were really soft. Right about in the middle she opened her mouth a little bit and without even deciding to or intending to, I put my tongue in her mouth and touched hers. She didn't seem to mind. She ran her tongue lightly along mine, back and forth. One problem I have is, I get excited very quickly with girls. Maybe everyone does. And maybe they do too, but they don't show it, which gives them an advantage in a way. Also, I didn't know how far she wanted to go. I wish girls would just tell you that, before you even started. She'd made all those remarks about certain boys not being her type or being gross, and I didn't want to seem that way. So we just kissed for a long time. I hoped she wouldn't notice that I had an erection.

"The thing is," she said very softly, "my parents will probably come back in around one second."

"Okay." I cleared my throat.

"Do you like me?" she asked. "Do you want to go out again?"

"Sure," I said.

She hesitated a second. "Do you have a girl friend at school?"

I shook my head. "The school I go to is just boys."

"Oh. . . . So, how do you meet girls?"

"I don't that much, I guess."

"Our school *has* boys," Leda said, "but the thing is, if you've known them since they were three and not even toilet trained, it's a little hard to feel romantically about them."

"Yeah, I know what you mean," I said.

"Anyhow," she went on, "it's hard to find someone you

30

like, but at the same time you're attracted to. It seems like usually it's one or the other."

"I know."

"Did you ever?"

"What?" I said. I kept hoping my erection would go away by the time her father came home. I didn't want him to think I was a sex maniac or anything.

"Ever find anyone, meet anyone who, you know, you liked, but you were also attracted to?"

I thought about that awhile. I guess the closest I ever came to that was this girl at camp, Lassie Bligen. She was a CIT in the Publications Shop, like I was, and wrote really good poetry, which they used to print in this magazine the camp put out. People always used to joke around about her name being Lassie. They'd bark when she came into the room and stuff like that. She did have shaggy blond hair, sort of like a collie, which hung over her face when she was sitting at one of the typewriters, working. I guess I always thought she'd be mad if I disturbed her. She looked so intent. But one day she came up to me and said how much she liked this story I wrote for the magazine. It was kind of a weird story about a guy who went crazy and thought the drink dispenser was God. I like writing stories like that. She said she thought it was terrific and I had a lot of talent. That night there was a camp movie and I asked her if she'd go with me; she said yes. Like I said, they tried to discourage sex as much as possible at our camp. That night, just for an example, they showed the movie *Fame,* but they made all these changes, some of which didn't make sense. (I'd seen it in the city so I could compare the two versions.) Like when somebody was supposed to say "tits" they say "jugs" instead. And when this dancer says about this guy, "I dig his Black ass," they changed "ass" to "butt." "Shit" became "shoot," and any similar words that couldn't be changed without really messing everything up were muffled. It was really dumb.

After the show we went off in the woods and started making out. Boy, if I'd only known she liked me a month earlier! It was, like, three days till the end of camp. We made out a few more times after that, but then camp was over. And she lived in California, of course, and the next summer, this past summer, she didn't come back to camp. If I ever go to California, I'm planning to look her up.

"There was this girl at camp from Los Angeles, Lassie," I said. "She wrote poetry." I looked at her. "How about you? Did you ever like—"

"Sort of," Leda said. "He was this actor. He was in one of the plays at my father's theater. The only thing was, he was, like, somewhat older than me, twenty-one or so, and he'd been married and Daddy thought I was too young. Maybe fathers always think that, his being married and all. I mean, he was divorced, but maybe Daddy was afraid he'd try and seduce me or something. You know the way fathers are."

"Did he?"

"What?"

"Try to," I said. Maybe that was a rude question, but she'd brought it up. And I was curious how much experience she had had.

For a minute Leda didn't answer, which I was sure meant he had, but finally she said, "Not exactly." She looked at me with a flustered expression. "It's sort of a long story. I'll tell it to you some other time. But, like, I'm a virgin, if that's what you want to know."

"Oh," I said. I guess I was pretty transparent. Girls seem to be able to read your mind sometimes. I didn't know what to say, whether I should tell her that I was too. I know most girls want you to have had more experience than they've had. Also, this actor must've had quite a bit if he'd been

32

married. He must have done it millions of times, at least with his wife and maybe other people too, actresses. Anyway, I was saved by the bell, so to speak, because just then there was a knock on Leda's door.

"That's Daddy," she said, jumping up.

❦ 5 ❦

Leda's father was short and chunky. His hair was completely gray. He looked a lot older than my father. "Want a ride?" he said. "I've got the car."

I told him where I lived. "It's kind of a long way from here."

"No problem. . . . It's getting late, Lee."

"I know, Daddy," Leda said. "We were just waiting for you."

In the car Mr. Boroff said, "So, how'd you like the play?"

"It was good," I said.

"Leda says you like the theater."

"Well, I . . . I guess I'm more interested in music."

"What do you play?"

"The electric guitar."

He shook his head. "Why does everything have to be electric these days? They're trying to make us all deaf, I guess."

"It doesn't have to be loud," I said. That's a popular misconception that a lot of people his age have. "You can play it any way you like."

"Yeah? . . . I like classical guitar, myself. Ever listen to Segovia?"

"Sure." That's the kind of music my parents like.

"So, that's what you're going to do? Be a musician?"

"I'm not sure," I said. "My father thinks it's not such a reliable way to make a living."

He laughed. "Fathers always spoil the fun, don't they? All that practical jazz about making a living. It's like Leda with her acting. Sure she's talented. So what? So are nine million girls. So, if she's lucky and gets a few breaks, she'll get a few parts till she's thirty. . . . After that, what? Lady Macbeth? I mean, look at my wife. She's a fine actress. I say that totally without prejudice. I'd have married her if she couldn't act to save herself, but she's good, varied, what have you. . . . So this winter she has to schlepp out to Seattle, Washington, for four months just to play a role in some half-baked play. Why? Because that's the only place that offered her a decent part . . . Seattle, Washington!"

I don't think my father would like it if my mother went away for that long. "That's a long time to be away," I said.

"Listen," he turned to me. We were at a stoplight. "We've been married thirty years. We don't go to pieces if we're apart four months. . . . It's for her. What's there to do in Seattle, Washington? You ever been there?"

"No," I said. "I guess the closest I've been to there is Los Angeles. That's where my brother lives."

"What is he, an actor or something?"

"He's a dental surgeon," I said. "But a lot of people whose teeth he pulls out are movie stars."

35

"Actors are the worst," he said gloomily. "I mean, you need them for plays, obviously, but unreliable!" He whistled. "So, you're going to college next year like my Leda? I told her—get an education, be well rounded. If, by the time you're twenty-two, that's all you want to do—go to it."

"My father would like me to go to Yale," I said. "That's where he went."

"And you?"

"I don't know."

I was afraid I shouldn't have told him that, that he might not approve, but he just said, "I never graduated college. Tried it. Two years. Never liked studying, so I quit. I've read everything you ever heard of, but I'm the type that operates on their instincts. It's always worked. So I figure—what could an education have done for me?"

That was surprising. I guess he's the first adult I ever met who didn't give me a big spiel about how college was the high point of their life. "I'd like to go to Paris," I admitted, "before college."

"You know French? Not that it matters. You'd pick it up."

"I know it pretty well," I said. "I've studied it four years at school."

He sighed. "Paris is a great place. . . . Great girls. I was there after the war. They all came running out in the streets, little dark-haired girls with big black eyes, hugging us. That was great. The war was shit, but that was great."

I couldn't think of what to say. "What war was that?" I said finally.

He burst out laughing. He had a deep booming laugh. "What war was that? I love it. You kids. . . . The Second World War. Ever hear of that one?"

He must have thought I was a real moron. "Sure I've heard of it," I said. "That was the one with the Nazis."

"The one with the Nazis. . . . Oh, I love you kids."
We were at my building.

I got out of the car. "Thanks very much for driving me home," I said.

"It was nothing. . . . Hope we'll see you again."

I hope I didn't make a bad impression on Leda's father. He seemed like an interesting person, even if he did have some of the same prejudices my father does about music. But about Paris, he was good. I wish he'd talk to Dad. Not that Dad would care if the girls there were great. I'm not sure how interested in women my father is. I mean, naturally, he's somewhat interested since he married my mother, and they seem basically happy, as parents go. But he never makes remarks about them the way Berger's father does. Berger's father, if we're going somewhere with him, will sigh and say, "God, will you look at that ass? They ought to frame it. It's perfect." Stuff like that.

In some way I wish Leda hadn't told me about that actor. Or I wish she'd told me the whole story. The whole story may be nothing special. Maybe she just had a crush on him and her father broke it up before it got off the ground, so to speak. The trouble is, he was probably extremely handsome. Most actors are. And, even if he wasn't married, he probably had around nine million girl friends, like my brother. She did say she was a virgin, but Berger claims girls can lie about that. If they think you wouldn't like it if they've had experience, they'll lie. I don't know if I'd mind if Leda wasn't. The only good thing about her being one, if that's true, is she won't be that critical.

Boy, this is really typical. Here I'm assuming we're going to do it and we've only been on one date! I did have the feeling she liked me, though. I guess I better ask Berger how to proceed next. I really don't want to screw this up by doing something dumb like moving too fast . . . or too slow.

Sunday morning I went over to Berger's house. I figured I could play tennis with Hope and maybe talk to him too. About sports, on a scale of one to ten, I'd put myself maybe at a six. I'm not a real jock, like some guys at our school who talk about nothing but sports and don't seem to care about anything else. I'm on the soccer team and I'm good. Plus my tennis game is not bad. Berger says the whole thing is a crock of shit and he refuses to learn any sport except Ping-Pong. He's fantastic at Ping-Pong. I know what he means, but I also think one reason he's not in such good shape physically is that he never gets any exercise. He also smokes quite a bit when his parents aren't around. Every time Hope finds cigarettes around the house, she knows they're his and flushes them down the toilet. He gets really mad, even though she's only doing it for his own good. He keeps trying to find hiding places where she won't find them.

"He's still sleeping," Berger's mother said.

It was noon. Berger loves to sleep. Sometimes he sleeps all day.

"I went in there and gave him a shove about an hour ago," Mrs. Wolfson said. "Go in and shove him again."

Berger's mother is really pretty. She has the best figure of any mother I know. I think Hope gets her looks from her. She's thin, with long legs and blond hair that she wears loose to her shoulders. I don't know how I'd feel having a sexy mother like that. My mother isn't bad-looking, but her hair is partly gray and she's not the kind men turn around to look at in the street. With Berger's mother they do. She doesn't mind. Once Berger and I met her after school to get tickets for a rock concert and when we got there, she said, "Hi, boys. This nice man has been trying to pick me up." The guy was really embarrassed; he turned bright red.

Berger's mother said, "I told him I had a teen-age son, but he wouldn't believe me. Aren't you my son?" she asked Berger. "Sure," Berger said.

When I went into Berger's room, he was lying in bed, but his eyes were open. "Okay, so how was it?" he said. "Close the door, okay?"

I closed the door, thinking he wanted privacy because of what I was going to say. But he said, "Joel . . . Could you go into the bathroom and look at the bottom of the hamper with all the dirty clothes? There's a pack of cigarettes down there."

There was. He lit up. "So, was I right?" he said.

"What?"

"About Blondie . . . Is she hot?"

"Oh, come on," I said, getting angry. "It was just our first date."

"So?"

"She's nice," I said. Suddenly I didn't feel like talking about it that much. "I like her."

"What about—"

"We went back to her place and made out a little bit, and then her father came home."

Berger shook his head. "Their fathers *always* come home. They're like watchdogs. . . . I wish I'd meet a girl who was an orphan. Or maybe whose parents were divorced and she was living with her mother who was a night nurse or something."

"She said she was a virgin."

"They always say that."

"So what. . . . You automatically think it's not true?"

"It *could* be true. Anything can be true."

"I think maybe it's true," I said.

"Well, for your sake I hope it's not, kid."

"How come?"

39

"Because then you have to go through a whole sturm und drang about mad passion and how you'll die if she won't do it. If they've done it with a couple of guys, it's more 'Wanna fuck?' and they either do or they don't."

I shrugged. The room was beginning to really stink from cigarette smoke. I could see some roaches crawling around near Berger's guinea pig cage, which he never cleans. "I didn't tell her I was," I said. "Is that okay?"

"What'd you—lie?"

"No, I just didn't say."

Berger sat up. "You can get mileage either way. Some of them figure that if you've never done it, it's because you're really choosy and you're waiting for 'someone special' quote unquote. . . . Not that you've been beating the bushes and haven't found anyone."

"I guess I'd rather be truthful."

He grinned. "So, when's your next date?"

"I don't know! That was just last night. I—"

There was a knock on the door. "Joel?" It was Hope. "Yeah?"

"Are we going to play tennis? You said we were." She opened the door just as Berger tried to crush out his cigarette and put it under the bed.

Hope marched over to him. "I'm not going to go to your funeral," she said. "I won't! So just remember that!"

"Okay . . . I'm not going to have one anyway. I want my ashes to be scattered over the reservoir."

"Well, if you die of smoking, I'll just flush them down the toilet," she said. Boy, she could really get mad.

"Give me a break, Hopie," Berger said.

Hope turned to me. "Tell him it's bad for him," she demanded.

"It's bad for you," I said.

We went over to sign up for a court. We had to play later,

at four, so I went home first. It was a little embarrassing playing with Hopie. She isn't bad, considering she's so little and only had six lessons, but she is a bit wild. If you play in Central Park, there's a whole row of courts, maybe twenty of them, and the ball can roll down a whole bunch of courts. Then you have to yell, "Court Ten, could you return the ball?" Usually they're too far away to hear you so you keep yelling, which disturbs all the courts near you. Also, since most people play with yellow balls, it's hard to tell which is yours and which is theirs.

"You could teach me how to serve," Hope said. She was wearing shorts and a Mickey Mouse T-shirt.

"I really think you should learn all that stuff from a pro," I said.

"I don't like him," Hope said.

"Why not?"

"He keeps telling me I'm not hitting it right."

"Well, but that's what lessons are for," I said, "so you can learn the right way."

She pouted. "I think you serve good. . . . Why don't you just show me?"

Actually, it's easier to teach someone to serve the right way than it is to do it. "The toss is really important," I told her. "I usually toss it too low."

Hope was looking at me. "Maybe you have an inferiority complex," she said, squinting up at me across the net. She had a yellow visor on, over her hair.

"What?"

"You keep saying you don't do things the right way, but you do! . . . I read about that in a book."

Hope reads a lot, sometimes ten books a week, Berger says. I climbed over the net. "Hopie, watch me, okay? Now try and toss it."

She got the idea of the toss pretty well and actually, I

41

wasn't sorry to slow down. If you play against someone who doesn't know how, sometimes they just can't get it over the net. But sometimes they hit it all over the place so you do more running than if you were playing a match. Toward the end a man called to me from behind the fence at the back of the court. "Hey, sonny."

"What?" I walked over to where he was standing.

"That's not allowed," he said.

Even though I didn't know what he was talking about, I got scared. My heart started thumping. "What isn't?"

"This court isn't for giving lessons. If you want to give lessons, you have to sign up, you have to register."

"He's not giving me lessons," Hope said. She'd come up behind me so quietly I hadn't heard her. "He's just showing me how to serve."

"Those are the rules," he said. "You want to stay out of trouble, you better check inside."

"He's my brother," Hope said.

"Honey, I don't care what he is. . . . I'm just telling you the rules, okay?"

By then the whistle had blown and we had to stop playing.

"That man was dumb!" Hope said angrily. "And I don't like men to call me honey. Neither does Mom. She says it's sexist."

"It may be a rule," I said. I felt flustered.

"Rules are stupid. . . . You're just as good as that man who gives me regular lessons." .

When we got back to their house, Berger was up. "So, did you lick the pants off him, Hopie?" he said.

"She's good," I said. "She can really move, unlike other members of your family."

"Joel showed me how to serve," Hope said, flopping down on the couch and kicking off her sneakers.

"You call that a serve?" Berger said.

Hope smiled at him, happily. "He's going to be my coach."

"Terrific," Berger said. He saluted me. "Hi, coach."

My father says women have more determination than men, that when they set out to get something, nothing gets in their way. Maybe that's true.

❧ 6 ❧

When I got home from school the day after Rosh Hashanah, my mother was sitting on the floor of the living room crying. There were a couple of things that were strange about that. First, my mother is hardly ever home before six. Her gallery closes at five and it's down in SoHo. A lot of times she has to have a drink with a client and doesn't get home till eight. The second thing is, my mother hardly ever cries that I can remember. She's what I guess you'd call a composed person.

"Are you okay, Mom?" I said, standing in the doorway.

She looked up. "Oh, Joel." She started to say something, but I couldn't hear what it was.

I went over and sat next to her. I put my hand on her shoulder. "What happened?" I said. For a second I thought maybe my father'd gotten run over or something.

"This is silly," she said. "I'm overreacting."

"What happened?"

"Gerald died," she said.

"Who's he?"

"Gerald!" she said, like I should have known. "Gerald Finn."

"You mean the guy you used to be married to?"

She nodded. "He was eighty-two, it isn't that it was premature, but I just didn't . . ." She took a deep breath. "And he left me these wonderful books in his will, these beautiful art books that he collected. For me!"

I better explain this. See, my mother was married to someone besides my father. She was only eighteen or nineteen and he was, like, thirty years older than her. He was her art professor in college. It's weird, if you think about it. I mean, my mother married to someone who's older than my grandfather! He was probably one of those little old men you see sitting on benches in Central Park or being wheeled around by some nurse. There's a man like that in our building. He lives with his daughter and her husband who are my parents' age. Mrs. Rees, that's his daughter, once told me he was married fifty years, his wife's dead now and he can't even remember her. It's good she's not around or I bet she'd be mad.

Anyhow, with my mother, I think she was only married to this guy a couple of years. Then she met my father. Maybe she started thinking about what it would be like later on, I don't know. But it isn't like she's kept in touch with him or talked about him a lot. In fact, usually I forget she was ever married to someone else because it happened such a long time ago. I wonder why he gave her all those books.

"How come he gave you those books?" I said. Mom was standing up now and looked basically her normal self, except her eyes were a little red.

"I don't know," Mom said. "I'm so touched, Joel. It's

not just that they're valuable, but he knew how much I loved them; he remembered, even after, even after . . ." She looked like she was going to cry again.

"Even after what?" I asked.

"I left him!" she said, sniffing. "I ran off with Franklin."

That's my father, Franklin. "That was sort of a long time ago, Mom," I said.

"I know," Mom said. "That's what I mean. . . . After all those years . . . And he didn't bear any grudge. It's so amazing."

My father came home early too. I guess Mom had called him at his office because he usually doesn't get home till six either. Some kids don't like that, coming home and finding no one there. I think it's good. I love being all by myself. Sometimes I go into my room and close the door anyway, but I never wish there were lots of people roaming around, like at Berger's house.

We all had dinner together. Sometimes, if my parents are eating late, I just cook something for myself, spaghetti or something like that. I'm a vegetarian. I forget if I mentioned that. I've been one for three years, ever since Mr. Hosei showed us this movie in Social Studies about how they slaughter cows. That's one movie I'll never forget as long as I live. My father says cows will be killed anyway, and that great cooking is based on meat. I wish he'd watch that movie. He might change his mind. Mom is a little better. She tries to get fish and chicken more than she used to. Sometimes she forgets and they have steak. I don't care, but I just won't eat with them those nights.

"Darling, I guess I don't quite understand," Dad said. "I think it's such a nice thing for Gerald to have done."

"I know!" my mother said. "And here I've hardly *thought* of him for years. . . . and I treated him so badly."

"You didn't treat him badly," Dad said, pouring himself another glass of wine. They have wine every night, even with hamburgers. Dad says it's not a meal without wine.

"I left him, I betrayed him. . . ."

"He was thirty years older than you, Mom," I said.

"Right," Dad said. "How could that have lasted? If anything, he took advantage of you, of your youth and inexperience."

"What do you mean?" Mom said angrily, putting down her fork. "In what way?"

"I mean, he used the fact that he was your professor to snow you with all he knew about art, he gave you a long song and dance about how miserable his marriage had been—"

"But it *was*," Mom said. Her cheeks were bright pink. "He was miserable! Frank, his wife used to bring lovers home and they'd be there when he came home from work!"

Dad sighed. "Okay, forget the taking advantage part."

"I don't know how you can *say* something like that," Mom said. "There I was, lonely, hating college, and he was the one person who was kind to me, who tried to show me a way out, who gave me confidence in myself. . . . And how did I reward that?"

There was a pause. "So, should we not have gotten married?" Dad said ironically.

"Of *course* we should have gotten married!" Mom said. "That has nothing to do with it."

"I seem to be emerging as the villain in this," Dad said. "Abducting this gentle young thing from—"

"You did," Mom said.

"Darling . . . You wanted to. I didn't—"

"That makes it worse!" Mom said. "I *know* I wanted to!"

Dad looked at me and smiled awkwardly. "I have a great

47

idea," he said. "Let's all go out for ice cream, how about it? Clear the air."

"You go," Mom said. "I don't feel up to it."

"Should we bring you back something?" Dad said. You could tell he was trying to get her calmed down, in a good mood.

Mom shook her head.

Dad and I went down in the elevator together. Dad sighed. "Oh, Christ," he said. "Gerald Hartley Finn."

"I can't imagine Mom married to someone who was eighty years old," I said.

Dad looked startled. "He wasn't. . . . He was forty something, I think."

"She said he was eighty-two."

"Oh, you mean now? Sure."

"He might've been like Mr. Rees," I said.

"Not all elderly people are like that," Dad said, "but you're right. I think Nan's forgotten why she left him. He was a domineering, selfish, uptight son of a bitch."

"Really?" I said. I wonder why Mom married someone like that.

We went into this terrific ice cream place near our house. I got a hot fudge sundae and Dad got a dish of burnt almond ice cream. Dad likes this place because they make everything fresh. He hates Carvel and Baskin-Robbins and chains like that.

Dad burst out with a funny laugh. "I ask you—do I look like someone who would abduct someone else's wife?" he said.

"What?" I said.

"The unreliability of memory."

"I thought you met Mom after she was divorced."

Dad shook his head. "We met at a party. I was the bartender."

"The bartender?" That was hard to imagine, my father

48

hanging around in a white apron making martinis for people.

"I was twenty-one, just out of college. No dough. Kind of floundering about what to do next in my life. A friend said this wealthy couple needed a bartender for a big party they were giving. So I figured why not. I bought a book on how to mix drinks. I was afraid people would come up to me and ask for tequila sunrises and Bolshoi punches. Actually, most of them just had straight Scotch or Bloody Marys."

"So, Mom was at the party?"

"No, she gave it, she and Gerald. I remember I rang the doorbell and this girl answered, wearing a red dress, her hair loose. I thought for sure she was the daughter. She said, 'I'm Mrs. Finn.'"

"Was her husband, like, really old?" I said, trying to imagine it.

"Not especially. The distinguished type, graying temples, custom-made suits, even a vest maybe. The whole thing overwhelmed me, though, a nine-room apartment on Park Avenue, antiques. I thought they must be millionaires! Actually, they *were* well off; Gerald had money from his family, but not the way it seemed to me then. All *my* friends were living in furnished rooms with kitchens in the living room. In my apartment the bathtub was in the kitchen, if you can picture it."

"How come?" I asked. I never heard of an apartment like that. What if one person was taking a bath while another was making dinner?

"They couldn't figure out where to put it. It was a railroad flat, a walk-up. So this seemed like real elegance and then this gorgeous young woman married to this old man—he seemed old to me then, though he was probably younger than I am now. . . . Anyhow, I just kept staring at her all evening. I couldn't figure it out, why she'd married him, what she was doing there. I thought she must have married him for his money."

"Did she?" I can't imagine Mom doing that.

"No, not really. . . . It was what I said. He snowed her with all this culture, quote unquote. He didn't lunge at her like the men she met in college. He was urbane, sophisticated, God knows. Anyhow, toward the end of the evening she came over to me. She said, 'You've been staring at me all evening. Is there a reason?' She seemed nervous. I said, 'Why did you marry him?'" Dad laughed. "When you're young, you say those things. I figured, what did I have to lose? I thought I'd never see her again. She turned bright red and walked away. I was scared they might not even pay me for the evening, that she was going to kick me out on the spot. But when the evening was over, she took me aside and gave me the money. I started to apologize. I said, 'I'm sorry about before, that was dumb. It's just you're so beautiful.' She just looked at me a long time. Then she said, 'I teach at Nightingale-Bamford. It's a school for girls on East Ninety-second. . . .' I went home and all of a sudden, while I was lying in bed, it came to me. She'd told me where she worked, so if I wanted, I could see her again."

"Did you?" This was really an interesting story. My father usually doesn't talk that much about himself. I thought they just met at a regular party.

"I showed up there at three o'clock the next Monday."

"Yeah, and?"

Dad smiled. "And we fell madly in love and she left poor urbane old Gerald in his paisley vest and we got married."

"Did she get divorced first?"

Dad laughed. "Yeah, she got divorced first." He sighed. "The point is, Christ, Nan was his third wife! The first one killed herself. Maybe he didn't drive her to it, but she did. The second one screwed around. So, okay, he was devas-

50

tated, but he remarried a couple of years later. And after Nan left him, he found someone else."

"How come he didn't leave those books to his wife?"

Dad frowned. "I think she died too, some kind of accident. Also, he may have had a soft spot for Nan. She loved art. He opened up new worlds to her, culturally speaking. Who knows."

He got up and we started back home. "I think she's probably calmed down by now," I said.

"Sure." After a minute Dad said, "Where are we going to *put* all those damn books?"

"Search me."

"I guess we could put them in Knox's room. I wonder how many of them there are."

Since my brother went to college, my parents use his room as a guest room. When he lived here, it was always kind of a mess, but now it's pretty neat.

When we got home, Mom was in the living room, reading. She looked more cheerful. "Hi," she said. "Was it good?"

"I think they're falling off a little," Dad said. "Something wasn't quite right with the burnt almond."

"Oh, Joel, Leda called," Mom said.

"Leda," my father said, closing his eyes. "What a beautiful name. . . . Does she have a long, graceful neck and milky white skin?"

My mother looked at my father. "Darling, being raped by a swan doesn't give someone a long, graceful neck."

"Doesn't it?" my father said. "I guess you're right." From the way he kissed her, I gathered things were okay between them again.

I went into the kitchen to call her. I told her about what had happened with my mother and the books and how my parents met.

51

"Boy, that's so romantic," she said. "My parents just met at work or something."

I guess it's romantic. I didn't think of it that way so much. "How are things going?" I said. We talk every night on the phone now and we've been out three times since I went to the theater with her.

"Okay. . . . Oh, hey, listen, Danny can go to the Simon and Garfunkel concert. Can Berger come?"

"I'll ask him," I said.

"It's going to be terrific," she said.

After we hung up, I called Berger and asked him if he'd go. "Sure, why not?" he said.

"Danny's for you," I said, just to remind him.

He laughed. "No poaching on your territory, huh? Don't worry, you can trust me."

"I'm not worried," I said. I'm not. Leda says she likes me and I believe her. I like her a lot too. It isn't just that we make out or that she's pretty, both of which are true. It's that she's really good to talk to about things. I found out she's a vegetarian too. She has this cookbook *Diet for a Small Planet* and she can cook lots of interesting, exotic things. She said one night when her parents are out, she'd have me over for dinner. She says her parents are really terrible about her being a vegetarian. They eat meat almost every night and her father sort of ridicules her. Like, she has this photo of a cow up in her room, a cow named Ali she took care of once on a farm. Her mother said it was ridiculous to put up a photo of a cow and took it down, but Leda put it up again. She says my parents sound really understanding, by comparison.

"So, what's the deal?" Berger said. "Do I call the dark-haired one or what?"

"No, they'll come together," I said. "They're going to get there at ten in the morning."

"Does she talk?"

"What?"

"Danny, Danielle."

"Sure, she talks. . . . Look, I don't know. Leda says she's very nice, but shy with boys."

"Shy meaning she hates them or what?"

"Berg, will you just go? . . . You'll see what she's like when you get there. What do you have to lose?"

"True."

I think Leda said her parents would be away that weekend, that they were going to Boston to visit some friends. That would be great because my parents don't go away that much. But I better not start fantasizing too much, just play it slightly cool.

❧ 7 ❧

It was hard finding them. There must have been a couple of hundred thousand people at the concert, most of them around our age. Leda had said they'd be over by this large tree, at one side of the Great Lawn. It took us more than half an hour to get there.

They were lying on a blanket. Danny was reading and Leda was standing up, looking around. "I got scared you wouldn't find us," she said.

She was in jeans and a bright pink T-shirt with some kind of dinosaur painted on it. The T-shirt was kind of tight. I saw Berger looking her over pretty carefully. "That's an ichthyosaurus," he said finally.

"Nope, a stegosaurus," Leda said.

"Huh, I thought I knew my dinosaurs." He sat down

next to Danny. "Hi," he said. "I think we met at the movies."

Danny looked up and smiled. She has a nice smile. "I remember," she said.

"What're you reading?" he said. "Anything good?"

She showed us the cover. "It's about this girl who had to, like . . . It's about incest. It's a true story."

"Heavy," Berger said.

"She was traumatized for life," Danny said earnestly, "and even when she grew up and got married, she still had all these nightmares. And she didn't want her father to come to her wedding, but he came anyway and got drunk. . . . It's really a sad story."

"I don't like sad stories," Leda said. "They're too depressing."

I sat down next to Leda. "Are you hungry?" she said. "We brought all this food, but we got hungry and ate it."

"We passed a stand back there," I said. "I could get something."

Everyone gave me their orders. I got hot dogs and a soda and some popcorn for Berger. He eats the most unhealthy things of anyone I know. As we were eating, he took out a pack of cigarettes and started to smoke. He offered them around, but no one took one.

"That's bad for you," Danny said.

"I know," Berger said. He smiled at her. "All good things are bad for you."

"That's not true," she said seriously. "Books aren't bad for you."

"Sure, they are," he said. "They pervert your mind, all that dirty stuff about girls making it with their fathers."

She turned red. "It's psychological," she said. "It makes you learn about human nature."

Danny does have big breasts. Now that Leda has talked about it so much, I couldn't help noticing. She was wearing a shirt that was a little big, but you could still see them when she bent over or anything. it seems strange that someone would want to have an operation to have them made smaller. Maybe she just says that to Leda because she's not as big. I think Leda has a good figure, but she's more on the slender side.

The concert was good. I know their music already because my brother has a lot of their records. Most of his records he took with him, but he gave me some he wasn't that interested in anymore.

When it got dark, Leda lay down with her head in my lap and her eyes closed. With Berger and Danny around, I tried to concentrate as much as I could on the music.

Danny said, "I feel funny."

"What's wrong?" Leda said.

"I guess I ate too much junk before."

Berger looked at her uneasily. "Do you think you're going to throw up?" he said.

"I don't know." She made a face. "I guess I better try and find a bathroom."

"There's one down there," I said. I'd passed it on my way to get the food.

"Do you want me to come with you?" Berger asked.

"No, I'll be okay." She walked off.

"We had, like, a lot of stuff before you came. . . ." Leda said. "Eggplant sandwiches and grapes and this bag of chocolate chip cookies and—"

Berger laughed. "Stop. *I'm* starting to feel sick."

"I hope she's okay," Leda said with a worried expression.

Ten minutes later Danny still hadn't come back.

"Maybe she got lost," I said.

"Her mother didn't even want her to go to the concert," Leda said. "They're really strict. They wouldn't let her wear makeup or date until she was fifteen."

"I'll go look for her," Berger said, getting up.

"Do you know where the bathroom is?" I asked.

"I'll find it."

When we were alone, Leda came over and put her arm around me. We started kissing. "Maybe we should have come by ourselves," she said softly.

"We can go back to your house afterward," I whispered.

"Yeah." She looked up. "God, look at that couple. That's gross."

About six feet away from us this couple was under a blanket. Maybe they weren't actually fucking, but they were certainly doing something similar.

"How can people do that?" Leda said. "That's rude."

"Yeah," I said. Watching them made me feel horny. I don't think I'd want to do it in front of a couple of hundred thousand people, even if I was under a blanket.

Leda stared at them. "Do you think they're going to finish by the end of the concert?" she said. Then she laughed. "God, I wish they'd stop. They're making me so horny."

It's funny that girls use words like horny. I never thought they did or that they talked about sex that much. "I know what you mean," I said.

"Do you think they're really doing it?"

"I don't know. . . . It sure looks like it."

All of a sudden the girl under the blanket said, "Oh, Joel, oh . . ."

Leda started to giggle. "She's calling you," she said.

Then, about five minutes later, they sat up and started listening to the music. Every time Leda looked at them, she started to laugh. I did too. I couldn't help it. "Oh, Joel," Leda whispered into my ear, imitating the girl. "Oh, oh . . ."

"What happened to Berger and Danny?" I said. I felt excited, even though she was just doing it as a joke.

"I don't know," Leda said. "Maybe they both got lost."

"Will you keep it down," the guy who'd been under the blanket yelled over to us. "We can't hear."

"Why don't you start fucking again?" Leda said, really loudly. Around ten people near us turned around and stared at her. The girl who'd been under the blanket looked extremely embarrassed.

"God, I'm awful," Leda whispered, her head on my shoulder. "I'm crazy. What a thing to say! . . . Joel, what do you think *did* happen to them?"

"I don't know," I whispered. "Maybe I should go look for them."

"What if *you* get lost?"

"I won't." I have a very good sense of direction.

I found the bathroom I'd passed on the way to get the food. Just as I got there, I saw Danny. She waved at me.

"Are you okay?" I asked.

"Yeah, much better."

"Where's Berger?"

"I don't know. . . . Isn't he with you?"

"He went to look for you."

"I didn't see him."

We looked around a little, but we couldn't find Berger. There were all these people leaning against the walls of the bathroom, smoking pot. This guy was walking around selling these long plastic things with fluorescent green liquid in them—glow-in-the-dark necklaces, or something. Anyhow, some people who'd bought them had nipped off the ends and were flinging the green stuff all over the place. They were all covered with glowing green spots. Danny and I decided we'd better move. So we went back to where Leda was and listened to the rest of the songs, but Berger never came back.

"What could've happened to him?" Leda said.

"I don't know." It crossed my mind that maybe he'd

picked up some girl and gone off with her, but I didn't say that. If that's what he did do, just go off, I'll be really mad at him. So Danny isn't his type? He didn't have to come if he didn't want to. But I didn't say anything to Leda or Danny. I figured they might consider me responsible since he's my friend. Like I say, Berger's sort of impulsive, not always, but he can be.

It took a long time to get out of the park after the concert was over. There were so many people, they had policemen guiding traffic on Central Park West.

"Do you feel okay now?" Leda asked Danny with a worried expression. You can tell they really like each other.

Danny nodded. "Pretty much. I think I'll just go home and go to sleep."

It turned out she lived about four blocks away so we walked her back to her building. Then we took the subway down to Leda's house. On the way Leda said, "I hope your friend is all right."

"He is," I said.

"How do you know? He could've gotten trampled to death. That happens sometimes with big crowds."

"I doubt it." I looked up at an ad for a bank loan. "He probably just picked up some girl and wandered off with her."

"How could he when Danny was his date?"

I shrugged. "He probably didn't."

"So, why'd you say that?" She looked puzzled.

"I don't know."

All I could think about actually was the fact that we would have Leda's apartment all to ourselves, that I could stay as long as I wanted. I was really eager to get there.

"When are your parents coming back from Boston?" I said as we went into her room.

"Oh, they didn't go," Leda said.

"How come?" I felt so disappointed, I could hardly speak.

"Their friends said it wasn't a convenient time."

I didn't say anything.

"What's wrong?" Leda said softly, coming over to me.

I hesitated. "I guess I was looking forward to . . . well."

"Yeah, me too," she said. She closed the door to her room. "They probably won't be back till late, though. They visited some couple out in New Jersey."

Still, it's not the same, not knowing when someone's parents are going to come home. They might, for some unexpected reason, have to get back earlier.

"Don't feel bad," Leda said. "They'll go away sometime."

"Sure," I said, trying to conceal how lousy I felt.

Then Leda did this amazing thing. I was sitting on the edge of her bed. She suddenly pulled her dinosaur T-shirt over her head, threw it on the floor, unhooked her bra and threw that on the floor and got out of her jeans. She was just wearing a pair of bikini underpants with little strawberries on them. She looked at me and struck a pose, her hand on her hip. "Ta da!" she said. "Preview of coming attractions."

I was stunned. I couldn't believe it. I guess she thought I was disappointed in the way she looked because she said, "I'm sorry I'm not that big, like Danny." She meant her breasts.

"You're perfect," I stammered. I was sure her parents would walk in the door that second. Leda came over and sat down next to me.

"I'm not perfect," she said. She smiled. "But I guess I'm okay." She looked at me. "You could take something off."

"My socks?"

"Sure, maybe your watch, even."

I took off everything except my underpants. I felt crazed with nervousness. I just hadn't been prepared for anything like this. We lay down on her bed and started kissing, the way we usually do. But it was completely different. I could feel all of Leda's body, everything. It was like she didn't have anything on. I let my hands run over her, except under her bikini underpants. I was afraid she might not like that. Her breasts are great. She's wrong. They're perfect. Everything about her is perfect! There was only one bad thing. I was sure I was going to come. I tried thinking of something completely unsexy, like the paper I had due for History next week, but it didn't work.

"Do you want me to touch you?" she whispered.

"Sure," I said.

She slipped her hand under my underpants and put it on my cock. She touched it gently like she was afraid it would hurt me or something. "Is that okay?" she said.

"Yeah, it's great." I was having trouble talking. I was scared I might pass out or something. Then she began stroking it up and down. It's funny. In a way, it wasn't as good as when I do it myself because if you've jerked off enough, obviously, you learn how to make yourself come pretty quickly. But the fact that it was Leda doing it made me so excited, I felt like I was going to go crazy. I tried to move to one side when I came because I was afraid I'd get the junk all over her hand. She didn't move away, though, afterward. She just lay in my arms quietly. I couldn't think of what to say.

"I hope I didn't mess up your bed or anything," I said finally. That sounded stupid.

"That's okay."

I took a deep breath. "I love you," I said.

"Me too," Leda whispered. "I mean, I love you too."

Then we just lay there, not saying anything. But it was a

good, comfortable silence. The phone rang. Leda has her own phone in her room. She got up to answer it. I watched her walk across the room. She's beautiful, she's perfect. This sounds strange, but I was scared if I stopped looking at her she would vanish into the wall and I would wake up at home in bed.

"Oh, hi," she said. "What happened to you? We were really worried. . . . What? Which hospital? . . . Is it serious? . . . Yeah, he's here. Do you want to speak to him?" She put her hand over the phone. "It's Berger."

I went to get the phone. I felt a little funny walking across the room without any clothes on, but it was pretty dark, half dark, anyway. "Where are you?" I said. "What happened?"

"St. Luke's," Berger said. "I twisted my goddamn ankle."

"How?"

"I tripped over a beer bottle."

I laughed, which may have been slightly heartless. "How?"

"What do you mean how? It was there and I didn't see it and I tripped over it."

"Did it hurt?"

"Of course it hurt, dope. I mean, I'm not mortally injured or anything. They just bandaged it up. I'm going home in a minute, but I thought I'd let you guys know, in case you were sitting around worrying about me." He laughed.

"I thought maybe you'd seen some girl and gone off with her."

"Thanks a lot. . . . Just walk out on Danny?"

"Sorry."

"I called her to explain. She was really nice, even though I woke her up. . . . Okay well, I don't want to disturb you. Go back to whatever you were doing, reading *Crime and Punishment* or whatever."

I'd told Berger about expecting Leda's parents to be away. I laughed. "Don't trip over any more beer bottles," I said.

"Don't worry."

I sat down next to Leda. "He's okay," I said. "It's not serious. . . . He called Danny to let her know what happened."

"I'm glad it wasn't just that he, like you said, wandered off. . . . She was afraid he might not like her because he's always joking around and she's not so much that type."

"No, I think he liked her."

"She once had this boyfriend who Berger reminds her of and he was kind of mean to her. Like, she thought she was pregnant? And he thought she did it on purpose to get him to marry her. He sounded awful."

"How could she have been pregnant?" I asked. It was funny having a conversation with both of us almost naked. I tried as hard as I could just to talk as though it was a regular conversation.

Leda laughed. "What do you mean, how?"

I cleared my throat. "Well, I mean, did they—"

"Yeah."

"Oh."

"You sound sort of shocked."

"No . . . I just, she doesn't seem like the type."

"What do you mean?" Leda said indignantly. "What type?"

"She just seems sort of shy, not that experienced."

"She isn't, really. . . . That experienced, I mean. It was just this one guy. It was—he was this carpenter who used to fix things at her parents' country house. And she kind of grew up knowing him. He taught her how to mountain climb and ski and stuff and last summer they just started doing it. Her parents practically killed him when they found out."

That made me nervous. "Maybe we should get dressed," I said. "Your parents might come home."

Leda laughed. "My parents aren't like that; don't worry."

"What are they like?"

"Well, it's true my mother is a little. . . . She doesn't trust me all that much. Like, if something happens, she always decides it's my fault or that I didn't use good judgment. But Daddy isn't like that. He's good. . . . Did you like him?"

"What?"

"Did you think he was a nice person?" Leda said. She was fastening her bra.

"Sure," I said, sorry to see her breasts disappear.

She pulled her T-shirt over her head. "He's sort of a genius. . . . I mean, he didn't invent anything like Edison, but he has this incredible mind. He knows everything. You ask him about anything and he knows all about it." She hesitated. "Maybe you should go home before they get here. Do you mind?"

I shook my head.

She smiled that mischievous smile she has. "Were you surprised when I took my clothes off? . . . You looked sort of surprised."

"Well, yeah, I—"

"I just figured . . . I knew you were disappointed about them not going away. I was too."

"I kept thinking about it all during the concert," I admitted.

"Me too," Leda said, "especially when that couple, the ones—"

"Yeah."

We kissed good-bye for a long time. It's a completely different thing kissing someone if you've seen them practically naked and touched them all over their body. It's like in your mind is all of that, even if they have all their clothes on. It's like they'd opened up their head and showed you all their thoughts in a way.

Maybe her parents will go away next weekend. God, I hope so. Or maybe mine will. They don't that often, but occasionally they do.

❧ 8 ❧

My brother's getting married. He wrote us about it. He also enclosed a photo of the girl. Her name's Angelica Spivack. She's quite pretty, but not a knockout like most of the girls he's dated since college. She had long brown hair and blue eyes. She runs a funeral home chain. It was her grandfather's business, but her father sort of ran it into the ground. That's not my joke. That's how Knox put it in his letter. In parentheses he wrote (ha ha). That's what my brother's like. He can be pretty corny.

It sounds to me like a really strange profession. Knox said Angelica was at this old age home where my grandmother is, picking up some corpses, and she ran into my grandmother, whom she'd met before. She didn't tell her what she was doing there.

I thought my parents would be hysterical with joy at

Knox's finally settling down, especially my mother. But they weren't that much.

"Is she Catholic, do you think?" she asked my father during dinner. "Angelica Spivack."

"Sounds Polish or Czech," Dad said.

"Do you think she's practicing?"

"Till she gets it perfect," Dad said. He can make pretty corny jokes himself.

"Frank, don't joke. . . . It's serious."

"Darling, I haven't the vaguest idea. I would doubt it. Knox isn't all that religious."

"Yes, but she might make him convert. They always want their children to be raised as Catholics."

"Why don't we wait and see when we meet her," Dad said.

My parents, by the way, are Jewish, but in different ways. What I mean by that is my father's parents never went to a synagogue and used to make jokes about how they'd never visit Israel because there were so many Jews. Whereas my mother's parents made a big deal out of it. When my mother's father was alive, he used to take me with him to the synagogue on Jewish holidays and he had Passover at his house every year. Since he died, we don't do much about it. Dad says going to Woody Allen movies and eating bagels is all he feels like doing about being a Jew.

"She isn't that pretty," I said, reaching for another slice of bread.

"Didn't you think so?" Mom said. "I thought she was lovely."

"Well, I mean, she doesn't look like a movie star or something."

"Knox had sense enough not to marry one of them," Dad said.

"Why?" I can't see why that would be dumb, marrying a movie star. In addition to being beautiful, she'd probably be extremely rich, have her own swimming pool, lots of things like that.

"Beautiful women, extraordinarily, professionally beautiful women, are trouble," Dad said.

"Frank, what a sexist thing to say!" Mom said. "How about Susie Daniels?"

"Susie Daniels is not extraordinary," Dad said. "Though she's quite lovely, I admit."

"Well, what in the world *do* you call extraordinary?" Mom asked.

Dad thought. "In real life, you mean?"

"Right."

He took a sip of wine. "I call Davida Hirsh extraordinary," he said.

"Davida Hirsh!" My mother choked on whatever she was eating. "She's just . . . That's just her manner. She just oozes all over every man she meets. Sure, she has a gorgeous figure, but . . . what's so special about her face?"

Dad laughed. "Does she have a face?"

Mom shook her head. "Frank, really."

"Or what's her name," Dad said. "You know, the one who grew up in Baghdad."

"Abra?"

"Yeah, Abra. . . . Look at the wreckage she's wrought on the men in her life. One went crazy, one jumped out of a window, Herman is an alcoholic."

"She just has bad taste in men," Mom said. "And she's not even that pretty."

"My point was just," Dad said, "that I think Angelica Spivack is perfect. Nice-looking, but Knox won't have to lie awake at night trembling for fear someone will snatch her away."

Mom laughed. "Like you do, right?"

68

"I'm a nervous wreck," Dad said, but you could tell he was joking.

I don't care what they say. I thought Knox would marry a movie star. It seems really dumb to wait all those years and then pick someone who runs a funeral home and goes around picking up dead bodies all day. I don't see how it matters if she's Catholic or not. My parents aren't that prejudiced about most things. Anyway, we'll meet her at Christmas when Knox said they'd both fly in.

At Thanksgiving something fantastic happened. My parents decided to go to Washington the day after Thanksgiving. My mother has to look at some art objects there and they have these friends, the Druscels, that they said they'd stay with. Leda and I worked out this plan. My parents are leaving Friday afternoon. She'll tell her parents she's staying at Danny's for the weekend and come over here Friday evening, around suppertime, and stay till Sunday. I'm so petrified my parents won't go, I can't think of anything else. I've always had trouble with that in school, anyway, thinking of something other than what the teacher is talking about.

Even though I've been out with Leda every weekend since the Simon and Garfunkel concert, we haven't gotten much further than we did that night. I guess we've always been scared either her parents or mine would come back right while we were in the middle of doing it. You figure for the first time, you'd like it to be reasonably relaxed, if that's even possible. Part of me can't believe it's really going to happen. You think to get a girl to do anything sexy, you'll have to practice some long speech or go all out to convince her, and then she just does something like that! I didn't tell anyone, even Berger. He'd start joking around about it probably.

Berger still has to use crutches, ever since the time he tripped over the beer bottle. He said the funny part of it was

69

that he was lying there in incredible pain when a doctor came by, a real doctor who happened to be jogging.

"From a hospital?" I asked.

"No, she was just jogging. . . . She didn't even know there was a concert. Can you believe that? She said to me, 'What are all these people doing here?' "

I didn't even know it had been a woman doctor. He never mentioned that. "She must have been kind of out of it," I said.

Berger sighed. "She was gorgeous. I think I dreamed the whole thing."

I thought of the way I'd felt that night. "What happened?"

"She was great. She told me to lie perfectly still and she'd find a stretcher to get me to the hospital. She said the main thing was not to put any pressure on the foot. . . . So I kind of lay there in pain and around five minutes later she came back with these two guys who were carrying a stretcher. They were just there, in case stuff like this happened. They took me to an ambulance and drove me to the hospital."

"What happened to the doctor?"

"She came along in the ambulance. She was just in her jogging clothes. She said she wanted to make sure I was okay. . . . What's so unbelievably dumb is I never found out her name! My darn leg hurt so much, I could hardly concentrate on anything else. I think I kind of passed out in the ambulance.

"How old was she?" I said, trying to picture it.

"In her twenties, I guess. . . . Black hair, blue eyes. Christ, why the fuck didn't I get her name?"

"Well, but if she's in her twenties, she's not going to have time for you," I pointed out.

"You can't tell," Berger said. "Look at Marilyn Globerman."

70

"Well, anyhow, you *didn't* get her name, so you might as well forget it."

Berger looked gloomily out the window. "What I thought I might do is start jogging around the area. Maybe I'll run into her again."

"At eight at night?"

He sighed. "True, it may be a little tricky convincing my parents it's safe. But they're always after me to get more exercise. . . . I wouldn't really have to jog. I'll just buy one of those jogging outfits people wear and maybe jog for a few feet. Mostly I'll just look around and see if I can find her. . . . I could hang out outside hospitals too. I wish I knew where she worked at least."

"How do you know she was a doctor?" The whole thing sounded supremely harebrained to me, but when Berger gets an idea, it's hard to stop him. He has kind of a one-track mind.

"What do you mean, how do I know she was a doctor? How do I know I twisted my ankle? I was lying there and she came over and said, 'You seem to be in pain. I'm a doctor. Can I help you?' She *looked* like a doctor. You can tell. Kind of crisp and cool and efficient, like she could cut you open, take out your intestines, and then go out for lunch." He laughed.

"What's so great about that?"

Berger looked at me in exasperation. "Didn't you ever just look at someone and have an overwhelming desire to get them in the sack?"

"I—"

He looked dreamy again. "She had beautiful hands. Maybe she was a surgeon. She put her hands on my face and said, 'You don't seem to have any fever.' What a voice! She had this great, musical voice. Imagine being married to someone like that. Every time you'd get sick with anything, she'd know exactly what was wrong with you, she'd look after you. . . ."

"Are you crazy?" I said. "If she's a doctor, she'd be off looking after other people."

"Naw," Berger said. "Not her. If I was sick, she'd drop everything. She'd sit by my bedside night and day."

"Sure."

He frowned. "Listen . . . I'm not joking around. I'm going to find her, if I have to jog forever. Years from now they'll find me jogging aimlessly, over rocks, around trees. . . ."

"Go ahead. . . . Who's stopping you?"

Berger looked impressed when I told him about Leda's and my Thanksgiving plan. "She must be madly in love with you, I guess," he said in a disbelieving tone, lighting up a cigarette he'd found under the hamster cage. Sometimes he hides them in this big sack of hamster food, way down at the bottom where Hope won't look.

I shrugged.

"Girls like her never just do it. . . . They've got to be in love. What'd you do? What'd you say to convince her? That you had a year to live?"

I laughed. "Nothing."

"Nothing?"

"Yeah, she just . . . I don't know."

"And she's a virgin? There's something fishy here, kid."

"Well, she does like me a lot," I admitted, looking modest. "I like her a lot too."

"Sex gets you crazy," Berger said. "That's the one thing wrong with it. It makes you totally certifiable. Like with Marilyn Globerman? I swear, if she'd asked me to take a flying leap out the window, I'd have done it. It must fry your brains or something."

"I know what you mean," I said. I don't know *exactly*

72

what he means, because Leda and I haven't done it yet, but I can imagine it.

"Maybe I'll take Danny out," Berger said, "while I'm waiting for the lady doctor to rematerialize."

I looked at him. "Berg, listen, don't . . . You know."

"What?"

"It's just, she and Leda are really good friends, and if you, you know—"

"What's the problem? You think she's going to fuck with someone like me? She's the intellectual type. She'll never do it till college."

I wondered if I should mention what Leda had told me about Danny not being a virgin. I decided I better not. I did tell him about how Leda said Danny had an inferiority complex about her breasts being too big, how she was going to have them operated on to make them smaller.

"You're kidding!" Berger looked horrified. "God, we've got to stop her. She must be crazy."

"Evidently, all kinds of guys go after her just because—"

"Not me," Berger said. "I'm only interested in her mind. I wouldn't put a hand on her if you paid me."

"Berg, I mean it. . . . Will you not—because Leda will be really angry at me if you start something with her and then she commits suicide or something."

"Worry not," Berger said. "It'll be strictly platonic. . . . I'm saving myself for the lady doctor."

I wish I could believe him.

❧ 9 ❧

My parents don't have the usual kind of Thanksgiving. My mother's parents aren't alive anymore and she was an only child. My father's brother lives in Europe and his mother's in an old age home in California. So, they never have a whole pile of relatives over the way some families do. Usually they just have a few friends. Mom's best friend from college is someone named Manon Knobler and Dad's best friend is someone named Casey Knobler. I know that sounds unlikely, but it's true. Neither Manon or Casey has ever been married. Mom used to hope they might marry each other. I guess she figured neither of them would have to change their name. But they never did. They didn't marry anyone else either and they always seem glad to see each other at Thanksgiving, but then they never see each other till the next Thanksgiving. Mom claims it's Casey's fault.

At least that's what she was talking about while she was in the kitchen fixing Thanksgiving dinner.

"He just has this classic hang-up about women who are smarter than he is," she said. "It's so sad."

"I don't know that Manon is all that smart," Dad said. "She's just driven."

"She *is* smart," Mom said. "She's driven too, but that doesn't make her not smart. Anyway, why shouldn't she be driven? How else do women ever accomplish anything?"

Dad was chopping up cranberries and kumquats for a sauce. Even though he loves to eat, he hates to cook. It's strange. Like, he'll take courses on cooking just to understand the "theory" behind it, but in practical terms he's not much beyond hamburgers and scrambled eggs. "*You've* accomplished a lot," Dad said to Mom. "And you're not driven."

Mom put the sweet potatoes in the oven. "Of course I'm driven," she said. "How can you say that?"

Dad ate a kumquat. "It's a quality," he said reflectively. "I feel like Manon is always slightly—like she's had eight cups of coffee. She rattles."

"That doesn't let Casey off the hook," Mom said grimly.

"What hook?" Dad said.

"Hanging out with girls in their twenties at his age. It's childish. And after being in analysis all that time."

My parents like to talk. They really talk a lot. The trouble is, sometimes they talk about the exact same thing maybe twenty times. Like, they've had this same discussion about Casey and Manon since I was around five. But they don't seem to notice. All I could think about, frankly, was their going away the next day. I got panicked when Mom sighed and said, "I feel strange, light-headed almost."

"Lie down for an hour till they come," Dad said. "I'll keep an eye on the bird."

"Would you, sweetie?" Mom said, putting her hand on

his neck. "I just hope I'm not coming down with something."

I wish I was religious. If I was, I'd get down on my knees and pray that my mother is *not* coming down with something. Dad looked in the oven at "the bird." We never have a turkey for Thanksgiving, like most people. Dad says turkey is a "travesty." He blames turkeys on the Indians. Instead we have this thing called a capon. What it is is a castrated chicken. Evidently once you do that to them, they get very lazy and sit around and eat all the time so their meat is very tender. I think that's a pretty sick thing to do to a chicken. How would my father like it if he was a chicken and someone did that to him? I don't exactly believe in the theory that people come back as other forms of life, but if my father came back as a chicken or a cow, he'd be in big trouble.

"You could invite her over for dessert," my father said.

"What?" I said.

"That girl you've been seeing, Leda. Would you like that?"

I got scared. I was afraid somehow Dad had caught on about our plan. "I think she's going to Brooklyn to have Thanksgiving with her uncle's family," I said.

"We'd like to meet her sometime," Dad said.

"Uh, sure," I said.

"You seem to be seeing quite a lot of each other."

"Sort of. . . . Dad, I guess I'll go and finish my math homework," I said quickly, "before everybody comes."

I don't exactly know what my parents would think if they knew about Leda's staying over. Don't worry, I'm not going to tell them. I'm not out of my mind. There's a chance my father might think I was taking advantage of her. In fact, there's a pretty good chance they'd both think that. And, like I say, I don't know that my father is all that interested in sex so maybe the whole thing would seem strange to him.

He and Mom still do it. I know that. But I don't get the feeling it's a major thing in their lives. I could be wrong. Berger says he can hear his parents when they do it. He says his mother really makes a lot of noise. My parents' bedroom is way down the hall from mine so I don't know if I'd hear anything anyway.

I just lay in bed, praying my parents would go on their trip. Even if my mother's slightly sick, she could still go, as long as my father drives. As long as it's not pneumonia or anything. Actually, I wasn't lying when I said that about Leda's going to Brooklyn. It's just I wouldn't want my parents to meet her until after this weekend. It's not that I think they won't like her; I don't care if they do or not. But I'm just scared they might start to suspect something.

Thanksgiving went all right. Manon and Casey seem to get along, despite what my parents said. Maybe they just don't want to get married. Not everybody does. I think my parents assume because they're married, everybody should be. Berger says he's never getting married. He might live with someone if he really likes her. I think I might, but definitely not till I'm thirty. My brother says it's good to try a lot of girls before you settle down. I doubt I'll get a chance to try as many as he has, but the theory of it sounds good.

Friday morning at breakfast my mother said, "I feel a lot better. . . . I think I was just overtired."

"Good," Dad said. He looked into the refrigerator. It was all crowded with the leftover food from yesterday. "It looks like you won't starve," he said to me.

"Do you think you'll have enough, hon?" my mother said. "I froze some cheese lasagna in case you get sick of the leftovers."

"I'll probably eat at Berger's a couple of times," I said.

"You can come with us," Mom said suddenly. "The Druscels would love to have you."

Sometimes you really rise to an occasion. I was so cool it

was incredible. I stood there, actually pretending to consider it. "I'd like to in a way," I said finally, "but I've got a lot of homework to do, Mom."

"I understand," she said, "though the Druscels did say their daughter might be home from school this weekend."

The Druscels' daughter, Kitty, is someone I wouldn't be interested in if I were lying on a desert island and hadn't seen a human face in a year. She's a total airhead. She goes to this really snotty school where all they do is put on makeup and try to meet boys who have lots of money. You can't imagine how dumb she is. She's the kind of girl who thinks Burt Reynolds is really sexy. She paints her toenails gold. I won't even go on about her because it makes me slightly sick to think about it.

Finally, at around three, my parents were packed. I was a basket case, I admit it, but I was fantastic about concealing how I felt. I went to the door and said good-bye to them. I acted totally normal. But after they left, I felt sick, I was so nervous. I was sure their car was going to break down or maybe they'd be in an accident and have to come home. Maybe my mother would get sick and they'd turn back. My idea was to wait one hour until they were definitely on their way. I tried to meditate, but it didn't work. Between thinking about Leda and worrying about my parents' car breaking down, I was a nervous wreck.

At four I called Leda's house. We'd planned that. Our plan was to say nothing on the phone that would sound suspicious. Leda's phone doesn't have any other extension—it's not the same number her parents have—but still, we decided it was best to be on the safe side. It rang a long time. Finally someone answered it and said, "Hello?"

It was her mother. My heart sank. I was sure she'd found out. "Uh, is Leda there?"

"Is this Joel?"

"Uh huh."

"She went down for about half an hour. Should I tell her you called?"

I tried to be as cool as I could, considering my hands were shaking so hard I thought I might drop the phone. "Yeah, it's nothing really that important," I said.

When I hung up, I felt so rattled. I didn't know what to do. How could she just go out? We'd planned that I'd call at four a couple of weeks ago and we'd gone over the whole thing a million times. What if Leda had changed her mind? What if she'd met someone at school? I was too jittery to sit still so I walked around every room in our house ten times at least. I pretended it was something I'd been ordered to do or I'd be shot. It wasn't very interesting, but I kind of got into the hang of it. I'd pretend to be whoever was giving the orders and say, "Nice work. . . . Just over that ridge a few more times, Lieutenant."

Just as I was circling my parents' bedroom for about the fifteenth time, the phone rang. I bolted into the kitchen to answer it. It was Leda. "Where were you?" I said excitedly.

"Oh, Mom just needed some milk from the store," Leda said calmly. "Everything okay?"

"Fine, all clear," I said. "When're you coming over?"

"Six thirty?"

"Great."

After I hung up, I wasn't sure what to do. I didn't feel like circling the apartment for another hour. In one way, I felt a lot less nervous than I had before I spoke to Leda and had been afraid she might not come at all. On the other hand, I felt a lot more nervous, knowing she was. What I did was I went into my parents' bedroom and got out their copy of *The Joy of Sex*. They don't hide it away or anything. It's right there. In fact, I've read it pretty much cover to cover several times. I always put it right back where I find it, which is between two novels, *Man's Fate* and *To the*

Precipice. I wonder if my parents ever read it. Sometimes I just look at the drawings if I'm feeling horny. The woman in the pictures is okay, but not outstanding, and the man is really ugly. I don't know why they drew someone with a beard. Berger suggested it was to show that sex can be great for everyone, even people who don't look like movie stars.

There are various passages I know by heart, almost. One says that sexual love is the "supreme human experience." It says it can also be "a bit hazardous" and can "give us our best and worst moments." Boy, I hope this is one of the best moments. How can it be that bad? I remember Knox saying when he first did it, he thought, *Big deal, what's all the fuss about?* I can't imagine being that blasé. In another part of the book they say, "Male sexual response is far brisker and more automatic; it is triggered easily by things, like putting a quarter in a vending machine." That's not such a great image, but still, I know what they mean. According to Knox, the key thing is not going too fast, but he never really explained how. I guess if you've done it hundreds of times, you're not that excited. You figure, *Well, just another fuck.* But how about the first time?

The trouble was, leafing through the book, knowing Leda was going to come over in less than an hour and maybe stay for the whole weekend, made me about ten times more manic than before. I started worrying that the second she'd get out the door, her mother would call her and force her to stay home. I imagined her getting run over as she got off the bus, or even getting raped on the subway. I have an overly vivid imagination at times. When the phone rang, I let it ring a couple of times because I wasn't sure I'd be able to talk. "Hello?" I said finally.

"Oh, hello, Joel? . . . Is Nan there?"

It was one of my mother's best friends, Louise Parker. "No, she's . . . she went away," I stammered.

"Went away?"

"She and my father went to, uh, Boston, I mean, Washington for the weekend. They'll be back Sunday."

"Oh. . . . Well, could you tell her I called?"

"Sure."

"Are you spending the weekend by yourself?"

"Pretty much," I said.

"Well, listen, if you get lonely, just drop over. Billy's coming in from Choate. I know he'd like to see you."

"I think I'll be pretty busy," I said, "but sure, I'll remember about it."

The Parkers live right near us and their son, Billy, who's my age, used to be a pretty good friend of mine till three years ago when they sent him away to boarding school. Since then, I haven't seen him that much. Berger hated him because he was kind of a jock (and a jerk).

About ten minutes after that, the doorbell rang. I'd given up on *The Joy of Sex*. Everything in it made me either insanely horny or maniacally worried. I opened the door. It was Leda. She was in jeans and her red jacket. She was carrying a blue bag. God, she's so pretty! Her cheeks and the tip of her nose were red from being outdoors. "So, here I am in all my glory," she said, grinning.

"Am I glad to see you," I said, closing the door quickly behind her.

"Did you think I wouldn't come?"

"You name it, I thought it."

Leda began looking around our apartment. She'd never been there before. "It's nice," she said. "You have a lot of paintings."

Partly that's because of my mother's gallery. If there's a work she really likes, she buys it. We have these really gigantic modern paintings that cover almost one whole wall. Some of them are a bit strange. There's one of a giant cheeseburger, done as realistically as a photograph. "Boy,

81

I'm starving," Leda said, looking at it. "Should we eat here or go out or what?"

"We could eat here," I said. "There's some lasagna."

I know Leda loves Italian food. "Great," she said.

We went into the kitchen. I turned on the oven. Mom's lasagna happens to be sensational. "Did you make it yourself?" Leda said, watching me.

I was so nervous, I said, "Yeah . . . I like Italian food."

"Me too," she said, "but I can't make it at all. . . . Except spaghetti."

"We could have wine, if you want," I said.

"Sure," Leda said.

I took her to this room at the back of our apartment. There's nothing in the room but wine bottles, stacked up to the ceiling on all sides of the room in metal racks. There's an air conditioner set in the window to make sure the wine stays at the right temperature. My father is manic about wine. I happen to know he has some bottles that cost a hundred dollars. He saves those for people he thinks really appreciate food. Those are toward the back. I decided to take one of the ones toward the front that they use every day.

"Red or white?" I asked.

Leda looked stunned by the room. "Is your father an alcoholic?" she asked in a worried voice.

"No, he just. . . . He has a very finely tuned palate," I said. That's what my father says. I took out a red Italian wine.

"I've never gotten really drunk," Leda said. "Hard liquor always tastes sort of awful to me."

I poured some wine into two big wineglasses. My parents have these huge wineglasses. My father always just fills them half full. That's to let you smell the wine before you taste it. Leda clinked her glass against mine. "So," she said, smiling. "To us."

I nodded. "To us." I took a long sip of the wine, hoping after a while I would feel relaxed. I felt good, though. At least Leda's someone I know and like and I know she likes me. I can't imagine doing it for the first time with someone I just met, the way Knox did. He said he wasn't planning on it, but he was at a party and this girl seemed really eager so he figured why not.

We ate in the dining room. Leda asked if there were candles. "We might as well make it romantic," she said.

"Sure," I said. I took out the brass candlesticks and put some blue candles in them.

She looked at me a little shyly. "I brought this dress, only I couldn't wear it out of the house or my mother would've been suspicious. Should I put it on?"

"Yeah," I said. "I'm not that dressed up, though." I was wearing jeans and a shirt and a sweater my aunt knitted for me.

"That's okay," she said.

She went into my parents' bedroom while I got everything out for supper. I lit the candles. It looked nice. We're on the twelfth floor and there's a view of Central Park.

"So, what do you think?"

I turned around. Wow. Leda was wearing this dress, the kind you wear to a dance. It was pink, that kind of soft material with a neckline that came down so you could see the tops of her breasts. She had a pearl necklace on and she was wearing some kind of terrific perfume. "You look wonderful," I said, dazed.

"Do you like pink?" she said nervously. "Danny thinks it's too—conventional, you know? But I think I look good in pink."

"You look good in everything," I said. I went over and put my arms around her. We kissed.

83

"You taste of wine," she said.

"You too."

We sat down formally at the table. "It's funny," Leda said. "I don't feel that nervous anymore. Last night I couldn't get to sleep till around three. I kept worrying about all the things that could go wrong."

"I know," I said. But I wondered what things she meant. I wonder if Leda ever read *The Joy of Sex*.

Leda drank her whole glass of wine. I poured her some more. "I think it's good that we both never did it before, don't you?" she said. "I mean, it's like we're starting at the same place."

"What about that actor?" I asked.

"Ramon? What about him?"

"Well, you said you almost . . ."

Leda looked embarrassed. "No, we . . . See, he had done it a lot of times. He'd been married and everything. He was still married, which was what got Daddy so excited even though he was separated and hadn't even *seen* his wife for a whole year, but he never got his divorce papers."

"So, how close did you come to doing it?" Maybe this wasn't the time to cross-examine her, but I felt like I had to know.

"Well, we went to this place one night and we took our clothes off, but it didn't work."

"It didn't work?"

Leda cleared her throat. "He, like, couldn't get in . . . I don't know."

I never heard of that. "What do you mean?"

"See, I think he had all these fears based on my being a virgin and Daddy's owning the theater. He said I was too young, that he wanted to do it with someone who could teach *him*. . . . And maybe I didn't want to that much. It was more that he was handsome and such a good actor."

I panicked. I don't remember reading about that anywhere, about a guy not being able to get in, when the girl wants to and everything. I guess I must have looked funny because Leda reached over and touched my hand. "It'll be different with us, Joel," she said, "because we love each other. Don't worry."

"I'm not worried," I said. I finished my wine and poured another glass. It was great wine, a little sweet, but not too sweet. I did feel different, like all the worries were there, but somewhere a little far away.

Neither of us ate all that much. I guess we were both thinking about what would happen after dinner. We stood up and looked out at the park.

"You have a nice view," Leda said. Her arms were around my waist. Her head comes up to my shoulder. I could hear her heart beating.

I squeezed her hand. "Do you want to go inside?" I said.

This next part may sound dumb. I brought her into my brother's room. There were various reasons for that. One is that since Knox moved away, that room is really neat. My parents use it for a guest room so it's always got fresh sheets on the bed. Also, maybe I was thinking of all the girls Knox has scored with, all the action that bed has seen, as it were, as opposed to mine, where I've just jerked off a million times.

"You're really neat," Leda said, looking around.

I decided to tell her later that it wasn't my room. Then there was an awkward moment. She looked so nice in her dress, but the whole point was to get her out of it. I started helping her undo the buttons that ran down the back. "There are millions of buttons," she said softly.

I turned back the bed. There were light pink sheets with flowers on them. "Those sheets are so pretty," Leda said. I knew she thought I'd put them on on purpose, for her. I would've if I'd thought of it.

We got under the covers and began kissing each other. I'd

never seen her completely naked before. The hair between her legs is a darker color than her regular hair. It felt soft and fuzzy. We were rolling around, touching each other all over. Finally, I even put my hand inside her. She didn't seem to mind. In fact, about a minute after I did that, she whispered, "Why don't we . . ."

Okay, so I did a classic thing. I absolutely couldn't help it. I entered her and it felt so great, just the *idea* that we were really doing it, plus the feeling, just everything, that I came. There's no way on earth I could've held off. When I was finished, I lay there on top of her, embarrassed.

"Hey, Lee, I'm sorry," I said.

"That's okay . . . I just couldn't wait."

"What?"

"I felt so excited," she said. "I just sort of came before you even got in."

"Oh."

"It's probably because we had all that wine," Leda said.

I took her into my arms. She put her head on my chest, her hand on my shoulder. I could feel her hair touching me. I think *The Joy of Sex* is right. It's definitely a supreme human experience. In fact, I can't think of anything that's happened to me so far in my life that comes at all close. "Did you like it?" I said. They say you shouldn't ask that, but I wanted to know.

Leda nodded. "It was great," she said. "I hope I won't be a nymphomaniac."

"I don't think you have to worry," I said.

"Was it hard getting in?" she said. "Ramon said I was tight or something."

"Not at all," I said. That Ramon sounds like a total jerk. God, am I glad he didn't try harder. I know that's a selfish thing to say, but I am. "Lee, listen, there's one thing—this isn't my room."

"Whose is it?"

"My brother's."

"How come you wanted to do it in here?"

"I thought he'd bring me luck," I said. I felt completely relaxed all of a sudden. I've told Leda how Knox had all these girl friends.

"I don't *want* you to be like your brother," Leda said, worried.

"I'm not. . . . Don't worry."

"I *hate* it when guys are just interested in scoring, just to tell their friends or something. . . . Will you promise not to tell Berger?"

"Aren't you going to tell Danny?"

"That's different. I won't tell her to boast or anything, just because she's, like, my best friend."

"Berger's *my* best friend."

"But it's different with boys."

"It's not *that* different, Lee, but I won't tell him if you don't want me to."

She snuggled up next to me. "Should we wear pajamas or a nightgown?"

"I don't have a nightgown," I said, grinning.

"I don't feel especially cold, do you?"

"Not at all."

❧ 10 ❧

That weekend was definitely the best weekend of my entire life. Maybe it'll be the best weekend I'll ever have. I wouldn't be surprised. I wonder if Knox feels about Angelica Spivack the way I feel about Leda. I can't imagine it.

I showed Leda Angelica's photo. We didn't get a whole lot of sleep Friday night, as you can imagine. I wonder what people do when they're just married and they have jobs and have to concentrate on other things besides sex. The best thing would be if you were really rich and could just go around the world for a year and then come back and do regular things.

"She's pretty," Leda said.

"Not as much as you," I said. I told her how my parents hadn't seemed as delighted as I'd thought they would be.

"It could be because they think she might be Catholic," I said.

"Maybe they're afraid because Catholics don't believe in birth control, some of them," Leda said. "Like, that they'll have nine million kids."

My heart sank. I suddenly remembered birth control. I hadn't thought about it at all. I remember thinking about it once, way back when we were planning this weekend, but then I forgot. I figured Leda was on the Pill. I remembered that remark Berger had made in the movie theater about girls on the Pill. "Uh . . . did you use anything when we—" I blurted out.

Leda smiled. "Sure. . . . Do you think I'm crazy? I have a diaphragm."

We learned about those in Sex Ed. I think our teacher said they're 97 percent effective "if inserted properly." I hope Leda knows how to insert hers.

"When did you get it?" I asked.

Leda was wearing one of my pajama tops and her bikini underpants. I had my bathrobe on. It was almost noon and we were still having breakfast. "Well, that time with Ramon, where Daddy sort of caught on something might happen? He took me aside and said he didn't approve of Ramon at all and he thought it would be a foolish thing to do, but if I was going to do it, I might as well not get pregnant in the bargain. . . . So he told me about a place to go to."

That sounded really strange to me. Berger has said his father said he'll kill anyone who tries anything with Hope. I thought fathers were usually like that with their daughters. "Does he know *we're* doing it?" I asked nervously.

"Probably," Leda said calmly. "Oh, not about this weekend. . . . Don't look so worried, Joel, it's okay. Daddy's really broad-minded. I don't know if this is why, but he tells this story about how in the war he was captured and they were going to, like, shoot him? Only some guard let him go. He never knew why. . . . And he says since then he feels like he was given a second life and all the things people make a big fuss about don't seem all that important."

I was silent, thinking of that. Leda kissed me. "He thinks you're a really nice person too," she said.

In the afternoon we went out to see a movie, *E.T.* We decided to go down separately in the elevator just in case we ran into any people my parents know who might say something to them. Leda went down first. When I came out of the building, I didn't see her at first. I got scared maybe she went home. Then she jumped out and grabbed my arm. "Boo," she said and laughed. Then she said, "Why did you look so scared?"

"I was scared you might have gone home."

She looked puzzled. "Why would I do that?"

I guess it's that I still couldn't believe this was happening. All weekend I'd kept looking in the mirror. There I was, the same person, the same face. Why me? Leda could've had anyone she wanted, famous actors, anyone!

We had pizza out for dinner and came home around seven.

"So, what should we do?" Leda said when we'd taken our coats off. "Watch TV or something?"

I thought she was serious so I said, "I'll see if anything good's on," even though I felt disappointed.

"I was just joking!" she said, hugging me. "I can *always* watch TV."

That night we almost had an argument. It wasn't an argument exactly. Here's what happened. When we were in bed, fooling around, all of a sudden Leda took my cock in her mouth and started sucking on it. It's not that I've never heard of that or haven't spent many hours imagining some girl doing it to me. It's partly that I never would have suggested it and she just started doing it, like it was the most natural thing in the world. She was fantastic. The trouble was, she was so good that I got completely carried away and came in her mouth. One article I read said girls hate that, the taste and everything. But Leda just swallowed it. Then she lay back against me and said in this really pleased way, "Was that good?"

"It was great," I said. After a second I said, "Didn't you mind swallowing it?"

She shook her head.

Maybe I shouldn't have asked the next question. My father says never ask a question you don't really want the answer to. "Did you ever do that before?" I said.

"Yeah."

"Who with?"

"With Ramon, that guy, you know, the one . . ."

"A lot of times?"

"I don't know. . . . A couple."

I was silent. I know it seems hypocritical to object that Leda had done it before. Obviously she wouldn't have been so eager to do it or so good at it if she hadn't, but I still felt upset.

"What's wrong?" she said. "Didn't you like it? . . . We don't have to do it again, if you don't want."

"It's not that."

"What is it, then?"

At the risk of sounding like a total jerk I said, "I guess I wish you'd never done it before with anyone but me."

"But then I wouldn't know how," Leda explained in that down-to-earth way she has. "See, Ramon showed me how. He said lots of girls are scared of choking on it. But there's a way to do it, so you don't."

I hate Spanish guys. I know that's an extremely preju-diced remark, but I've hated them way before Leda started telling me about this Ramon. They always seem so sharp and sinister, like they're about to twirl their moustache and pick your pocket. "Did he have a moustache?" I asked.

"What?"

"Ramon."

"No." Leda paused. "He looked kind of like . . . You know Erik Estrada? From *CHiPs?*"

Erik Estrada is someone Hope adores. She even wrote him a fan letter, saying if he ever came through New York, he should stay at their house. He has muscles a foot in every direction, and in every picture I see there are girls hanging all over him. "Shit," I said.

"Joel, come *on,*" Leda said. "I'm in love with *you.* I don't want *him*. He was really shallow. He never read anything. He was just so full of himself."

He probably had a cock nine feet long. I just couldn't get that image out of my head, Leda sucking him off and him lying back enjoying it. I mean, why shouldn't he enjoy it? "Is it you're jealous or what?" she asked.

"Sort of," I admitted.

"Listen, I'm a virgin," she said and laughed. "Was. . . . Be glad of that."

"I *am* glad," I said.

"Why? What does it matter? That was then, this is now."

I know that's a good philosophy and I'm not someone who wants to marry a virgin. Knox says guys like that are Neanderthals. He says he wants someone who likes sex enough to have done it a lot. Of course, he's not the type to be insecure about whether one of the other guys was better than him.

After that it was good. I told myself—quit worrying. She likes you, loves you, even. So enjoy it while it lasts. The trouble was, I wanted it to last forever and I know most things don't, especially at our age.

Sunday we hung around in the morning. We watched cartoons on TV and took a shower together and Leda made

92

pancakes. I played Leda some of the songs I'd made up on my guitar. The trouble is, I don't have such a great voice, but she seemed to really like them. "They're just as good as Simon and Garfunkel," she said. "I bet you could make a record." I know that's not true, but it still made me feel good. It was only when we started cleaning up in Knox's room that I noticed there was blood on the bottom sheet.

"I guess the first time you do it, there's some membrane or something that has to break," Leda said.

I'd read about that, of course. Still, I felt slightly sick at the thought of her bleeding from something I did. *"Did* it hurt?" I said nervously.

"A little bit," Leda said. "It wasn't so bad."

I'm really glad I didn't notice the blood till now. "Did it hurt all the times we did it?"

"Joel, don't worry, please. . . . It hurts a little bit in the beginning, but it's not, like, excruciatingly painful. . . . Only maybe we better wash the sheets."

I didn't want to do it in our basement where they have washing machines, for fear of running into someone. So we took the sheets to this place on Broadway where you wait while they're being done. It's just one big room with giant washing machines in it. By then I was beginning to feel really exhausted. I'd slept around four hours all weekend. Also it was that feeling that here we'd had this incredible weekend, and it was over. It was like spiraling down from a tremendous high, maybe the way people feel after drugs. The weather was lousy out—cold and dark, even though it was only around two in the afternoon. Leda and I leaned against each other, watching the sheets go around and around. I could tell from her breathing she was falling asleep. She hadn't slept much either. I wonder why my parents have separate beds. I think, based on this weekend, that one of the major points of getting married would be to sleep in one bed. Maybe they're afraid they won't get enough sleep if they sleep in one bed.

I've never given a lot of thought to my parents' sex life. I wonder if my father did it with anyone except my mother and who they were and how much he liked them. Obviously, my mother did it with Gerald Finn, if they were married for three years. Though maybe they didn't do it too much since he was so old. When it comes right down to it, I don't know too much about what my father thinks about women or sex. I just remember once my parents had this argument. They don't argue much, at least not that I know about, but this was after some party. I was in bed, but not asleep. Maybe they thought I was asleep because they were really yelling. My mother was saying my father had been flirting "like a maniac" with someone at some party they'd been to and that if he ever did that again, she'd divorce him. "I saw you go out on the terrace," she said. "She was showing me their tomato plants," my father said. "Bullshit!" my mother screamed. "You were out there half an hour and it was pitch black." "Look, if I was going to have sex with someone other than you, I wouldn't pick Abra, for God's sake," my father yelled. "Who *would* you pick then?" my mother said, very sarcastically. I can't remember the whole conversation, but I do know that the whole next day my mother hardly spoke to my father at all. At dinner there was a real pall on everything. But then, by the end of the next week, everything was normal.

Berger says his parents have had some really wild fights. Once his mother bit his father on the arm so hard he bled and once he took some meal she'd fixed and threw it against the wall. My parents aren't the type to do that, no matter how mad they get.

I guess I must have fallen asleep too, waiting for the laundry, because all of a sudden I heard someone say, "Hey, what do you know? The great Joel." It was Billy Parker, the guy I mentioned whose mother called up Friday afternoon.

"Oh, hi," I said. Leda stretched and opened her eyes.

"Aren't you going to introduce me?" Billy said.

"Uh, Leda, this is Billy Parker. He used to go to my school."

I got mad the way Billy began giving Leda the eye. Berger's right, he *is* a jerk. I forgot because I hadn't seen him in so long. He always pretended to know a lot about girls, but Berger claimed it was pure imagination. He took a beer out of a paper bag. "Care for some?" he said.

Leda shook her head. "Where's your laundry?"

"Laundry?"

"This is a place to do laundry," she said. She got up and started taking our sheets out of the dryer.

"I just came in to drink my beer. My parents won't let me touch anything when I'm home, even beer." He must have noticed what Leda was folding up and put two and two together. "Your parents went away, huh?" he said to me. "Mom was afraid you'd be lonely, but I guess she didn't need to worry." He grinned broadly.

Leda was looking at him with an annoyed expression. I think he was already a little crocked. "So, what's a nice girl like you doing with Davis here?" Billy said.

"None of your business," Leda snapped.

"Hey, do you have a sister?" Billy said, not even seeming to notice her tone. "I think I met your sister at a party. She looks just like you only she has shorter hair."

"I don't *have* a sister," Leda said. She put the sheets in the shopping bag.

"Really?" He turned to me. "Does she really not have a sister?"

"Nope," I said.

"I don't know," Billy said. "I think maybe you have a sister, but you don't know about it. She goes to Andover.

Her name's Raphaela. I think she said her mother was Italian. Is your mother Italian?"

"Joel, I think we better get back," Leda said, pulling at my jacket.

"Nice meeting you," Billy called. He sat down in one of the chairs to drink the rest of his beer.

"Ugh," Leda said when were outside. "He was a friend of yours?"

"It was a long time ago," I said. "And we weren't that good friends."

We got the sheets back on the bed and then Leda had to go home. Usually my parents don't get home till six or seven, but we decided to be on the safe side. Anyway, like I said, I was so exhausted I was almost glad she was going home.

We kissed for a long time at the door. "It was a wonderful weekend," Leda whispered.

"You're wonderful," I whispered back.

"You too."

After she left, I fell sound asleep for about five hours. I didn't even hear my parents come home. When I woke up, it was nine o'clock. I heard sounds in the kitchen and knew it must be them. I washed my face with cold water and went into the kitchen. "Hi," I said.

They were having coffee. "Oh, hi, darling," Mom said. "You must have been tired."

"Well, I was up pretty late studying," I said.

Berger says his mother has an X-ray mind. He says she can look right at him and know if he's lying or not and what the real truth is. I don't believe in that, but I still felt funny. I wondered if I looked different to them. "Did you have a nice time?" I asked.

"Very," Mom said. "Louise Parker said Billy was in. . . . Did you have a chance to see him?"

"No, I didn't," I said carefully. "We aren't that good friends anymore, actually."

"She said he was put on probation for drinking," Mom said. "Goodness, at his age!"

I thought of the bottle of Dad's wine we'd used. We put all the garbage out, but I wondered if he'd notice it was gone. "Your lasagna was great, Mom," I said.

Mom looked pleased. "Oh, I'm glad. . . . I was worried you might not have enough to eat."

"Everything was fine," I said. "Great."

"I'm glad I don't have to worry about your being lonely when we go away," she said thoughtfully. "That's one of the advantages of your having been brought up almost as an only child. You have inner resources."

❧ 11 ❧

I'm going to do my father a favor. He and Mom insist that I apply to college, whether I end up going or not. They say they haven't ruled out my going to Paris, but they want a backup plan. So I told Dad I'd go up with him to Yale. The point, obviously, in *his* mind, is for him to show me around and get me so wild with enthusiasm that I decide to go there. I can't imagine anyone in their right mind preferring New Haven to Paris, but it can't hurt to go for one weekend.

I called Leda to tell her I wouldn't be around. We'd been seeing each other every weekend since Thanksgiving so I know she counts on it. It was the second week of January.

"Oh, that's okay," she said. "Danny and I are going to this dance at school."

"What dance?" I said.

"You know, just a dance. . . . Doesn't your school

have them? . . . And we might go to *Rocky Horror* with a bunch of kids afterward. Danny's never seen it."

"But what if I'd been here?" I said, feeling slightly sick.

"Then you could have come," she said.

I didn't know what to say. Finally I said slowly, "I don't get it, Lee. . . . What's the point of going to a dance?"

"They're fun."

"Yeah, but aren't we . . . I thought we were going together."

"We are," she said impatiently, "but that doesn't mean I'm entering a convent. Anyway, I hate that expression 'going together.' It sounds so fiftiesish."

"Well, I guess you know what you're doing," I said curtly.

"Joel, come *on!* Nothing's going to happen. . . . What're you worried about?"

"I'm worried that nine million guys will make passes at you."

"So? I can duck. . . . Look, I love *you*. Why're you so insecure? The guys in my school are jerks, most of them. I just like dancing."

I'm not a very good dancer. I can do it, but I'm not terrific. "Well, have fun," I said.

I must've sounded sarcastic because Leda said, "I will! . . . I'll *try* to anyway." She sounded mad. "And I don't get this bit of trying to make me feel guilty. It's dumb."

"Okay."

I hung up feeling lousy. Mom and Dad claim the kind of dancing kids my age do isn't that sexy, not compared to the kind they used to do where you're pressed right up against someone. Maybe. But if someone like Leda in a miniskirt and tights is wiggling around, tossing her head back and forth, I know exactly what every guy there is going to be thinking. He may not act on it, but his thoughts will definitely not be one hundred percent clean. I wish Leda hadn't bought those miniskirts. She says it's a cute fashion. It is, in a way. But I wish her mother was like Danny's mother, who wouldn't let her get one because she thought it would make people think she was a slut and she might get raped on the subway. "Did you ever *hear* of anything so dumb?" was Leda's response to that.

I don't think it's that dumb. Maybe the getting raped on the subway part is. But the thing is, you should see Leda in her miniskirt. It comes just over her butt, maybe three inches, and she wears these very bright tights in various colors. Sometimes she wears these strange things called legwarmers, which are hard to describe—they're like crumpled up wool stockings. Or she wears her Frye boots. No matter what she wears, it's definitely a sexy outfit. I don't know if it would make people think she's a slut, but it certainly would make any guy in his right mind start thinking along a certain line. I'm not going to say any of that to Leda because when I have, she says I have a dirty mind and she'll wear whatever she wants anyway.

I did tell Berger about Leda and I making it together, by the way. It wasn't to boast, the way Leda was afraid it would be. It's just, Berg and I have been best friends for six years and he tells *me* everything. It wouldn't make sense for me not to tell him.

I went over to his apartment the day before I was going to drive up to Yale with my father. We walked home from school together. He was all excited about something he said he wanted to show me, but he wouldn't tell me about it till we got there. When we were in his apartment, he took me into his room, closed the door, and got a stack of Xerox copies out of the closet. He handed one to me. This is what it said:

*To the Sexy Doctor who saved my life
at the Simon and Garfunkel concert:*

*You were jogging. I was in incredible pain. You got me to
the hospital. You are beautiful and have long black hair.
I haven't stopped thinking about you for one second. My
friends fear for my life. Take pity on a desperate soul!
Call 555-4332 between 4 and 6.*

I just looked at him. "So, what're you going to do with
these?"

Berger looked really pleased with himself. "I'm going to
nail them on every tree in Central Park within a five-mile
radius of where I met her. I'll bury them under rocks!
. . . She's bound to find one."

"She'll think you're a maniac."

"No," Berger said. "She'll be touched. Her heart will be
wrung."

"Berg, this plan is so full of loopholes. You're going to
get nine million crank calls. And what if your parents
answer the phone?" Berger doesn't have his own phone
number.

He tapped his head. "I've got it all figured out. I let Hope
in on the plan. She's very romantic, you know. She'll be
here every afternoon, fielding calls for me. Hopie's sharp.
Anyhow, I'm not giving out my address. I'll just get her
phone number and call her back."

"Will you remember her voice? It was two months ago."

"Are you in love or not? Of course I'll remember her
voice! If I heard her voice when I was ninety-five and on my
deathbed, I'd jump sky high and go running."

I stared at him. "She's twenty-five, at least, if she's a
doctor, maybe twenty-six."

"So? Age doesn't matter. Women like younger guys.
We're at our sexual peak, remember?"

I sighed. "I don't know, Berg. . . . It's not going to work."

"So, what is? I've been jogging there every day. I've never seen her."

"Maybe she was transferred back to wherever she comes from."

"God wouldn't be so cruel."

"I thought you didn't believe in God."

"So? What's that to him? Even if I don't believe in him, he still may be up there, preventing things from falling totally apart."

There is no earthly way to talk Berger out of something when he's got it in his head. He is a monomaniac. I saw Hope as I was leaving. "He's crazy," I said.

"I think it's romantic," Hope said. She always finds a good way to look at anything Berger does. "I hope he finds her."

"I do too."

"Do you want to see me do a split?"

"Sure."

Her face lit up. "They put me in the advanced class. I'm the youngest one."

"You're great, Hopie."

She was staring at me in that fixed way she has. "Do you still have your girl friend?"

I nodded.

"Maybe you and Berger can go out on a double date, when he finds his girl friend."

"Maybe."

I wonder if what appeals to Berger is just that it's so hard to find this woman. He likes challenges. Maybe if he'd just met her in some regular way, he wouldn't have gotten so caught up in this. I wonder if he really does think about her all the time. I think about Leda almost all the time. Not on purpose. It's just I'll see something or someone will say something and it'll remind me of her. I dream about her quite a bit too. I don't have to tell you what kind of dreams they are. It's annoying in a way. You want to feel you have control over your thoughts, but at night, when you're asleep, your unconscious takes over.

Dad drove us up on Saturday. We got there in the early afternoon. He took me to the college dorm he was in, Trumbull. It looked nice, with the usual Gothic-type architecture. I was afraid Dad might do a whole number with showing me his room and going into an orgy of nostalgia about how college was the greatest time of his life, but he didn't. He was fairly quiet and self-absorbed-seeming. He drove me around, showing me various things, but it was basically low key. "I can't exactly sell you on New Haven," he said, "but it's close to New York. . . . And now that Yale's coed, you won't have any problems with a social life."

Leda has talked about going to Yale. Her SAT scores were a lot better than mine, but on the other hand her father didn't go there. I shouldn't say a lot better. She was in the 700s in math, and I was just in the 600s. We were about the same in English, 720 or so.

"So, what do you think?" Dad said.

"What?"

He smiled. "Are you too dazed by love to give a damn about college?"

I didn't realize it showed. "No, I'm not too dazed," I said coolly.

"When are we going to meet her?" Dad pursued. "You seem to be seeing an awful lot of each other."

"Sometime," I said. I looked out the window.

"How about next weekend when Knox comes home? He'll have his girl, you can have yours."

"Okay."

"She must like you a lot," Dad said.

"What makes you say that?" I said warily, turning to look at him.

"Well, she calls all the time."

"Yeah, well, it's basically mutual, I guess."

Dad was gazing ahead. "Just don't be a schmuck with women, Joel."

What a thing to say! "I wasn't planning to, Dad," I said dryly.

"No, I mean it," Dad said. "They're sensitive, there's no way around it. The good ones are sensitive. You have to treat them. . . . Well, you'll figure it out."

"Yeah, I'll figure it out." I wished he'd stop talking about it.

"I'll shut up in one second," Dad said. "Just one final thing. About sex. I don't care *what* the women's lib people say. Women take it more seriously than men. They can't help it. It's biological. So don't, if she's a nice girl and I assume she is, fool around and make her life miserable. Okay?"

"Don't worry, Dad." It's completely unlike my father to deliver Polonius-type speeches like that. I don't know what got into him.

After we drove around awhile, we went back to our hotel, the Taft. "Ah, the Taft," Dad said when we were in our room. "The scene of one of my few, furtive attempts at losing my virginity while at college."

I looked at him sideways. I didn't know he'd been that old when he lost it. "Who was she?" I said.

"She was, God, I'm totally blocking her name. I'll tell you what she looked like, though. She was tiny, five feet tall maybe, with fluffy blond hair. Adorable. Kind of scatter-brained . . . Joy. Joy to the World, my roommate called her. We'd met at some party, I don't even remember. I invited her down for a weekend and put her up at the Taft."

"So, what happened?" I said. I was really interested.

Dad was sitting on the edge of the bed. "We came up to her room. We made out a little. Everything was *much* slower in those days. And then she arched back her head and said in solemn tones, 'I'm much more neurotic than you can *possibly* imagine.' Well, the trouble was, she seemed pretty neurotic without my even thinking about it. I guess I decided trouble lay ahead, more than it was worth."

I would have liked to know who the girl was he finally did do it with, but I couldn't bring myself to ask.

Then we both took a nap. I felt really tired, maybe from being out of doors. When we woke up, it was after seven. Dad said he wanted to take me for dinner to some place he knew. "The food is not outstanding," Dad said, "but it's edible."

I'm not like my father. I can eat more or less anything, if I'm hungry. Actually, I thought the food was pretty good. I had fried clams with mashed potatoes and a salad. Dad said he was going to try the boeuf bourguignon, even though he knew it would be lousy.

"It's not all that bad," he said. He was having wine as usual. "Hmm. Not bad at all."

Just as we were finishing the main course, I noticed Dad staring over at some people at a nearby table. In New York when I eat out with my parents, they almost always seem to run into someone they know. But New Haven is a little out of the way. "I can't believe it," Dad said finally, "but I think that's Constance Gibson."

"Who's she?" I asked.

"Can it be?" Dad said. "God, I haven't seen her for thirty years! I just don't know."

"Who is she?" I said again.

"I think it's her," Dad said. "I'm sure it's her. That is incredible! . . ." He turned to me. "Constance Gibson. She was my girl friend."

"While you were at Yale?"

105

"Yeah. She was at Smith. Remember what I was saying before about being a schmuck with women?"

"Uh huh."

"Well, was I a schmuck with Constance! Connie. Oh, I cringe to remember it. Just picture this lovely, lovely girl, long legs, blond hair, big hazel eyes. She came from some little town in Illinois. Can you imagine? Wilderness! It wasn't till she was in high school that her parents had indoor plumbing installed. She milked cows! Sweet, innocent."

"So, how did you treat her like a schmuck?"

"Oh, I was always after her. I thought I was such a big deal because I was taking a couple of philosophy courses, because I'd read more than her. Over breakfast I'd read her Rilke, in the original. Jesus! She didn't know German, she'd never read a poem. I got her so upset about all she didn't know that she went home on Christmas vacation and she screamed at her parents, 'Why didn't you tell me about Rilke? Why didn't you tell me about Dostoevski?' She said her mother just looked up at her—she was probably sitting there in a gingham apron, churning butter!—and said, 'Dear, we didn't know.'" Dad sighed. "God, when I think of that scene! 'Dear, we didn't know.'"

That didn't sound so bad to me. I'd thought he'd meant more seducing and abandoning her when she was pregnant or something. "Should we get dessert?" I said. I still felt hungry. Mom sometimes calls me "the bottomless pit" because I can eat so much and not get fat.

"Joel, listen, would you mind . . . I just want to go over and say hello, okay? It'll only take a sec. You order dessert or whatever."

"Do you want anything?"

He shook his head and wandered off.

I watched him. I wondered if it was going to turn out to be the same person. Actually, it was two women sitting at a table, one about my mother's age, and one younger, like in her twenties. But if he hadn't seen her for thirty years, she might look a lot different. The waiter came over and I ordered apple pie a la mode. When I looked over at my father again, he was sitting down at the table, talking to the two women, so I guess he must have guessed right. I wondered how long he was going to stay there. My apple pie came and I ate it. It was good. I started thinking about Berger going around nailing all those sheets to trees in Central Park. I wonder if that's against the law. I hope he doesn't end up in jail. But now that I'm in love with Leda, I know that you can do really crazy things when you fall in love with someone, things you never would have imagined yourself or anyone doing. I don't know if I'd nail messages on trees, but I know what it's like to feel desperate enough to do something like that.

Dad came back to our table.

"Was it her?" I said.

He nodded. "Joel, I'd like you to come over and meet Connie. She's here with her daughter Meg who goes to the Yale Law School. They're very eager to meet you."

"Okay," I said. I didn't really have any choice.

Connie, the mother, my father's old girl friend, was pretty attractive for someone that age. She had blond hair, very neat, turned under, and big blue-tinted eyeglasses. She looked like the kind of sexy librarian or teacher or secretary in a movie who, somewhere along the line, falls in love with the hero and takes her glasses off and gets drunk. Her daughter wasn't as pretty. She could've been, her features were okay, but she had really bad skin. She had a lot of makeup on to cover it, but you could still tell.

"Well, hi, Joel," Connie said. She turned to my father. "He looks *exactly* like you, Franklin. I can't believe it. It's uncanny."

I guess her eyesight can't be too good. No one in their

right mind would say I look exactly like my father. There may be a vague family resemblance, that's all.

"This is my daughter, Meg," Connie said. "She's at the law school."

"Hi," said Meg, but in a kind of bored way. I wonder if Berger's right about women that age, in their twenties, thinking guys in high school are so great. This one looked at me as if I was just out of kindergarten.

"Franklin tells us you're applying to Yale," Connie said. She had this slightly breathless way of talking, like she'd been running around the room and hadn't had time to catch her breath. "I think that's marvelous. And now that it's coed—"

"Oh, Joel won't have any problems with girls," Dad said. "They call him up all the time. They're hammering our door down."

I glared at him. I decided it was beneath my dignity to reply.

"I love that," Connie said earnestly. "It's so healthy, girls feeling free to do all that, not caring about conventions! Remember how I thought I was such a wicked woman because I was six months older than you, Frank?" She turned to her daughter. "The rule was: The man must be older, smarter, taller. Well, of course, Franklin was brilliant. Those poems you wrote!" she said. And suddenly she quoted, " 'For I have eyes to hear and ears to see the footsteps and the running of the Gods.' "

Dad looked at her in amazement. "Did *I* write that?"

"Of course you did!"

"I think this is the high point of my life," Dad said, delighted. "You remembered that poem for thirty years?"

She looked indignant at his doubting it. "I used to know them *all* by heart, Frank. They were wonderful! Did you ever publish them?"

"No," my father said. "I just . . ."

This was really weird. I never knew my father had written poetry at all!

"And do you still write?" Connie asked.

"Oh, the occasional poem, if I feel inspired," my father said, "but just as a hobby."

They beamed at each other. Suddenly her daughter got up. "Mom, listen, I promised I'd meet Jimmy at ten. I'll see you tomorrow, okay?"

"Have fun, darling," Connie called. After her daughter had gone, she said to my father, "Frank, am I being terribly, *hideously* old-fashioned? I just worry *so* about this Jimmy. He's been married twice, he . . . And Meg is so vulnerable, such a darling, really."

"She *is* lovely," my father said. "Almost as pretty as you, Con."

Connie blushed red. "Oh, she's a million times prettier than me."

"Never," my father said. I began to wonder if he was drunk. I never saw him act this way. Then he turned to me. "Joel, I think maybe Connie and I would like to have an hour or two to talk, catch up on old times. Is that okay? Will you be all right?"

"Sure," I said. I'm not a baby, for Christ's sake!

"I'll take care of the bill," my father said. "Did you have dessert?"

I nodded.

Connie smiled at me. "I'm so glad we had a chance to meet, Joel. . . . I know you'll *love* Yale."

I went back to our hotel room. I felt really depressed. First, my father acting like such a jerk, then the thought of Leda being at that dance. I'd brought my guitar and tried playing it awhile, but I got exasperated. Sometimes I think I'm just not that good. If I didn't listen to records so much, maybe I wouldn't be able to tell the difference. Also, it's more fun playing *for* someone, especially someone like

Leda. After about fifteen minutes I put it down and turned on the TV. I thought it would be better to watch a stupid movie than just try to go to sleep and not be able to. I flipped from one channel to another. Each movie was stupider than the one before it. Finally, I just left it at the channel I'd started with first and lay down on the bed to watch it.

It's depressing watching TV in a hotel room, I don't know why. At home you can watch and study or stop and go into the kitchen and get something to eat. Here it was like being trapped. Then the movie itself started getting to me in various ways. It was about a teen-age girl who runs away from home and becomes a hooker and has various sordid and humiliating experiences before her parents find her and bring her home. The girl looked a little like Leda. Not exactly—actually I think Leda's a lot prettier—but she had that perky way of walking and that mischievous smile, head tilted a little to one side. I started feeling both horny and depressed, which is a lousy combination, believe me. There was one scene where the girl goes to a hotel room with a guy who wants her to do something she doesn't want to do. They were a little vague about what it was, but the girl got down on her knees and started crying, "Please don't make me do it, please, please." She was just wearing this very skimpy slip that was falling off her shoulders. Finally I couldn't take it anymore. I turned the set off, clicked off the light, and jerked off, imagining that scene, only with Leda and me as the main characters. By then I was kind of sleepy. I didn't fall right to sleep, but I must have eventually because I don't remember hearing my father come into the room.

When I woke up in the morning, it was eight thirty and he was sleeping in the bed next to mine. Outside it was raining, that kind of cold, horrible December rain. I took a hot shower. When I came back into the room, my father was up. He was still in bed, but he had his glasses on.

"So, how was your date?" I said.

"What date?" he said nervously.

"With Connie."

"That wasn't a date, Joel. . . . We were just—"

"—catching up on old times," I finished for him. "So, did you?"

"What?"

"Catch up on old times?"

"Yes, we did. . . . It's interesting. She's had a very different life from what I would have expected, from what *she* expected too, I gather. She married one man and he died very young of a heart attack. Thirty-two, I think she said. Some congenital thing. . . . And she went back to school, got a business degree, and is now working for a computer firm in Boston, doing pretty well, I gather."

"Did she remember that you were a schmuck with her?" I asked. I guess I was sort of needling my father. I just felt like it for some reason.

"No, it's amazing. . . . She had the most idealized memories of me," Dad said, getting out of bed. "A great poet, a great lover . . . God, the tricks memory can play!"

"Weren't you?" I said dryly.

"Not really. . . . Look, I was twenty. What does anyone know at twenty?"

"I thought men were at their sexual peak then," I said, thinking of what Berger had said.

"Oh, well, in that sense, but it takes time to—" he gestured. "Women are complex. Each one is different. You learn as you go along."

I had the feeling he didn't feel like talking about it anymore. Or maybe that was all he had to say on the subject. He went into the bathroom and locked the door.

At breakfast he asked, "So, what did you think of her?"

"What?" I was thinking of Leda, but in a more calm, relieved way now that the dance was over. Whatever had happened had happened by now.

"Of Connie?"

"She was okay."

"That corn silk hair!" my father said dreamily. "I think only girls brought up on farms in southern Illinois have hair like that. Incredible."

We drove home after breakfast. Dad didn't pressure me much about how I'd liked Yale. I guess he realized that would be counterproductive, as our Social Studies teacher is always saying. Actually, I liked it better than I thought. I still think I'd rather take a year off, but maybe when I get back, I could go there, *if* I get in.

We got back Sunday afternoon around three. I called Leda as soon as I could. Nobody answered her phone. Naturally, that made me feel not too great, but I was good. I sat down and for the next two hours I did my homework, listened to music, and didn't even think about her that much. Then, just before six, she called me.

"So, how'd it go?" she said, sounding very friendly. "Did you have a good time?"

"Yeah, pretty much," I said. There was a slight pause. "I called you before, but there wasn't any answer."

"Oh, God, Joel, Danny and I did the craziest thing! Should I tell you? Do you want to know?"

I wasn't sure I did, but I said, "Sure."

"Well—wait a sec. I want to make sure my door's really closed. . . . Okay. Well, we got these costumes of nuns that Daddy had from some play, real nuns' habits? And we put them on, only with them we wore these really high spike heels, three inches, and *tons* of makeup. Mom's in Seattle now, doing her play, and Daddy was out, so we went into her makeup cabinet and we lathered ourselves up with everything we could lay our hands on, green eye shadow and this gold stuff you sprinkle on your face to make it glitter and dark red lipstick, almost purplish. . . . And then we went to this movie. Only we waited an hour in the lounge, having coffee. You should have *seen* the conversations we had! This one man came over to us and said he wondered what order we belonged to because his sister wanted to join a convent and we seemed such modern young girls and so full of life."

"So, what'd you say?"

Leda giggled. "Oh, we made up all this stuff. God, I hope the Catholic Church won't sue us. We said we were from an order named St. Helena's which was on a remote mountain in Switzerland and we made our living pickling cherries and selling them and our special job was to milk a flock of snow white goats. He just believed the whole *thing!* He said he thought we sounded so dedicated and that was really special and we wouldn't ever regret having given up our lives to serve God."

"Didn't he think it was slightly strange that you were wearing shoes like that and all that makeup?"

"I don't *know!* . . . But later this slightly sinister guy came over to us and said, 'Hi, Sisters. How're ya doing?' like he knew something was funny. He said he was a policeman! We got so scared. We thought he was going to arrest us! So we went into the ladies' room and washed all our makeup off and when we came out, he was gone."

"How was the dance?" I said. I couldn't figure out any more subtle way to bring that into the conversation.

"It was okay," Leda said. "Nothing special. We couldn't go to *Rocky Horror* because Danny's mother didn't want her staying up so late. So we just kind of came home and made popcorn and stuffed ourselves."

After I hung up, I felt both much better and like kind of a jerk. Why was I so worried about that dumb dance? The fact that Leda told me about it ahead of time proved she wasn't going to do anything sneaky, behind my back.

At dinner my mother asked me how I liked Yale. I was in such a good mood I said, "It was great."

"Great?" Mom looked surprised. "I thought you'd find New Haven a bit drab after New York."

"No, we did a lot of interesting things," I said.

I wonder if Dad mentioned about meeting Constance Gibson. I wasn't sure so I didn't say anything about that.

❧ 12 ❧

I decided to do what Dad said—to invite Leda for lunch the weekend Knox was bringing Angelica home. She seemed excited about meeting my parents and a little nervous. "Do you think they'll like me?" she asked.

"Sure," I said.

Actually, what I was hoping was that they'd be so preoccupied with Angelica, who's going to be part of our family, that they wouldn't have time to focus on Leda. Not that I think they *won't* like Leda, but it's slightly less pressured than if I were to bring her just by herself.

Angelica Spivack looked pretty much like her photo. She had a really nice smile. There was a little gap between her two front teeth and that made her look natural; she hadn't even bothered to have it fixed. She was kind of skinny, not even as big on top as Leda. Knox looked sharp, as usual.

He's always tan, and his hair gets blond from being in the sun, so even though it's basically the color of mine, blondish brown, it looks more blond.

"We're so delighted to meet you," my mother said, hugging her.

For some reason my mother had been running around crazily, fixing the house up, afraid Angelica might expect something more glamorous than our apartment. "Angelica is such a pretty name," my mother said. "Is it after a saint?"

I guess she was trying to find out for sure if Angelica was Catholic.

"My mother just thought it was a pretty name," Angelica said.

We sat around in the living room waiting for Leda, who was late as usual. Angelica asked Mom if she had an ashtray. My mother gave up smoking ten years ago and doesn't like it when people smoke. She went into the kitchen and came back with the saucer from a coffee cup. "I'm afraid this is all I have."

"I only have six a day," Angelica said apologetically. "Knox has been so good. He nags at me like a fishwife if I have any more."

I told her about Berger and how he hides his cigarettes all over the house, so well that even he can't find them sometimes.

"It's a terrible habit," Angelica said. "I started in college. I got so nervous before exams!"

"Nan smoked like a chimney when I met her," my father said.

"Sweetie," my mother said indignantly. "I didn't! . . . I never smoked more than a pack a day."

"You did it so intensely, though," Dad said. "Oh, it was charming, in a way. You always seemed to be wreathed in smoke, like a woman in a veiled hat. It added to your mystery."

Mom looked at him sideways. "And now my mystery is gone?"

"Never," Dad said, smiling. "You're just as mysterious as ever."

The bell rang. It was Leda. She gave me her coat. "I'm sorry I'm late," she said breathlessly. "The subway just wouldn't come!"

"That's okay." I hung her coat up in the front closet.

"Do I look all right?"

I looked her over. There's not much you can say in answer to a question like that when there's nothing the person can do about changing. Actually, Leda looked gorgeous. Her hair was all fluffed out and her eyes looked big and sparkling. It was more what she was wearing that was— well, not what I'd expected. She was wearing a gauzy white blouse with lace on it and a very full patchwork skirt. She wasn't wearing a bra. Sometimes Leda wears a bra and sometimes she doesn't. She says she isn't always "in the mood" to wear a bra, whatever that means. It wasn't that her blouse was totally see-through, but you could tell she wasn't wearing one. It just didn't seem like the greatest time to have picked out not to wear a bra, meeting my whole family for the first time. But what could I say? I couldn't exactly whip into my mother's bedroom and get one, even if they wear the same size which I doubt. "You look great," I said finally.

"Is my eye shadow okay?" she asked. "I got this new color, Moonlight Blue."

"It's fine."

I took Leda into the living room and introduced her to everyone. Knox gave her the once-over in his usual discreetly lecherous kind of way. Dad smiled and said how happy he and Mom were to finally meet her.

117

"We've heard so much about you," Mom said. "Joel can't stop talking about you."

Why do parents have to act dumber than usual on occasions like these? It's not even true! The fact is, I may *think* about Leda a lot, but I hardly talk about her at all, certainly not in front of my parents. Mom said we could eat any time we wanted so we all went into the dining room.

It was one of those all-out gourmet meals that Mom does occasionally where Dad hovers around her in the kitchen, tasting things and, she claims, driving her crazy if he thinks the seasoning is off even a little bit. Dad poured wine for everyone, but Angelica said she didn't drink wine, that she'd have water instead.

"I guess you like wine a lot, Mr. Davis," Leda said. I was scared she was going to say something about the wine we'd drunk that night she spent the weekend, but she didn't.

"For me it's not a meal without wine," Dad said, for about the millionth time in his life. He began talking about some new wine he'd discovered and how great it was.

"Joel says your father owns a theater, Leda," Mom said when we were eating the first course, "and that you're interested in pursuing an acting career?"

"Well, kind of," Leda said. "I mean, he does own a theater, but they want to make sure I get a good education, my parents, I mean. They want me to go to a good college and then get training as an actress if that's what I still want to do."

"That's what *we* say to Joel," Mom said, beaming approvingly.

"I used to take acting lessons and it was, like, the only thing I thought about, so they made me promise to hold off till next year." Leda paused. "I really miss it a lot. I love acting!"

"*I* used to act in college," Knox said. He leaned over to Leda. "What have you been in?"

118

"Oh, gosh, well, I was in a couple of musicals. My voice isn't that great, but it was fun. We did *A Chorus Line* at my school last year and *Oklahoma!* the year before that."

"Who were you in *Oklahoma!?*" Knox asked.

"Ado Annie," Leda said. Then without any warning she started singing, "I'm jist a girl who cain't say no . . ." She only sang around two lines. She has a good voice, but I was really embarrassed. What a choice of something to sing!

"Gee, you're really good!" Angelica said. "I can't sing at *all,* or act. Not to save myself."

"Well, it's fun," Leda said—she seemed really relaxed, about a million times more than I was—"because you're not being yourself. That's what I like about it." Then she described how she and Danny had dressed up as nuns that weekend I was at Yale with Dad. She told it pretty much the way she'd told me. "I guess it was kind of an awful thing to do," she said at the end, "but it *was* fun."

There was a long silence.

Angelica had a strange expression on her face. "I think I . . . where's the bathroom?" she said and rushed out of the room.

Leda looked at all of us. "Did I say something wrong?" she said.

"Well, it's just Angelica went to convent schools when she was a girl," Knox said, "so she may be a little sensitive about—"

Leda cringed and clapped herself on the head. "Oh, God, how awful! Oh, how dumb! . . . Listen, I'm *so* sorry. Should I apologize? Should I say something to her?"

"It'll be okay," he said in his most suave, soothing voice. "Maybe I'll just go speak to her a minute." He left the room.

Leda turned to my parents. "I'm really sorry," she said. "Did I wreck the dinner?"

"Don't be silly," Dad said. "There was no way you could have known."

"See, my parents just aren't that religious," Leda said. "I mean, they're Jewish, but they're not that . . . So, like, I guess I never think—"

"I think it's mainly that she's a little nervous, meeting us," my mother said. "She and Knox are getting married, you know."

"Yeah, I know!" Leda said. "That's great!"

"We never thought he'd settle down," Dad said. "He has a little black book the size of the Manhattan telephone directory."

"Maybe he was sowing his wild oats," Leda suggested cheerfully. "Sometimes men like to do that, I guess. Or women too, maybe. Just so, like, when they finally do marry, they'll be faithful."

"I'm sure Knox will be faithful," my mother said. "He's a very kind, loving person at heart."

I don't think I'd be too sure of that, but I didn't say anything.

Eventually Angelica and Knox came back. She looked a little flustered. "I can't get used to the time change!" she said.

"Yeah," Leda said eagerly, obviously trying to make up for the previous incident. "Me too."

"Oh. . . . Aren't you from New York?"

Leda turned red. "Yeah, I am. . . . I just meant in general, it's hard to get used to. Like daylight savings and all."

Angelica got up to help my mother clear and Leda went into the kitchen with them.

"Angelica seems like a lovely girl," Dad said.

Knox smiled, a little ironically. "Thanks, Dad."

What I'd really like to know is what made Knox pick her

out of all the women and girls he's met. But he'd probably think that was a rude question.

"That Leda's a real cutie," Knox said, grinning at me.

I cleared my throat. "Well, she . . ."

Dad smiled. "A little hard to handle, I would imagine."

"They're the most fun," Knox said.

"Is Angelica hard to handle?" I asked sarcastically.

"Marriage is different," he said. "For marriage you want peace, understanding, not just fun and games."

I was getting really pissed off—Knox's implying that the only reason I was seeing Leda was "fun and games," Dad's implying that I couldn't handle her. If only she hadn't worn that damn blouse without a bra! If only she didn't talk so much!

I guess Leda and Angelica made it up in the kitchen because dessert went pretty smoothly. After dinner Mom and Dad said they had to go out to a cocktail party and then they were going to a movie. Angelica and Knox disappeared into his room. Leda and I went into my room. Somehow my room isn't that romantic. I'd straightened it up to some extent, but it's kind of small and ratty looking. I felt awkward about it and wasn't sure what Leda was expecting us to do. We sat down on the bed. She kicked her shoes off.

"I feel like they've taken our room," she said, in a slightly wistful voice.

"Yeah, I know."

She lay down on the bed and looked up at me. "What's wrong?" she said. "You seem like you're in kind of a bad mood."

"I'm not in a bad mood," I lied.

"Why don't you lie down, then?"

I did, but I just lay there, looking at the ceiling. "I don't get why you didn't wear a bra," I said.

Leda looked surprised. "It would have shown," she said.

"I tried it with a bra, but the straps showed. . . . Why, could you see my nipples or what? It's not *that* see-through." She looked down at herself. "I thought it looked pretty."

"It *did* look pretty," I said, but I still felt detached and angry.

"Are you mad because of that thing I said about the nuns? Your parents seemed so understanding about it."

"Not really."

"So, what's bugging you?" Leda said, beginning to sound angry herself. "I thought I was really. . . . At least I talked! *You* just sat there like a mummy!"

"Well, I guess you made up for both of us."

She sat up, cheeks flushed. "You didn't want me to talk? Were we all supposed to sit there and grit our teeth like that pasty-faced little clump your brother is marrying?"

"She's not a pasty-faced clump."

"I suppose you think it's so wonderful that she runs a chain of funeral homes?" Leda said, furious. "Well, I'll tell you something. I read this book about that once and those people are crooks and cheats! They go to poor, really *poor* people who don't have a cent to their name and they humiliate them into buying these expensive coffins they can't even afford. It's a racket! Poor people who don't even have *food* to eat!"

"She may not be like that," I said.

"I bet she *is*," Leda said grimly. "I bet she grinds every last cent she can out of them."

"You don't know anything about it." I sat up.

"I do!" Leda said. "I read a whole *book* about it!"

"No, I mean you don't know anything about her particular—"

"Okay, so you want to marry someone who runs funeral homes?" Leda said. "Go ahead! Maybe she has a younger sister."

"Lee—"

"Personally, I wouldn't marry someone like that in a million *years!* Because of her probably millions of families aren't even going to have lunch for months! Just because she's rich! Is *that* all you care about?"

"Yeah, that's all I care about," I said.

"How was *I* supposed to know she was Catholic, anyway?" Leda said. "She wasn't wearing a big gold cross around her neck."

"Her name's Angelica."

"So?"

I reached up and took her hand. "Lee, come on. Let's not argue. I'm sorry. I was just in a funny mood before."

Leda looked like she was going to cry. "I thought I looked *pretty,*" she wailed. "I asked everyone, my mother, my father, Danny, how I looked and they all said so! They didn't even notice I wasn't wearing a bra! Just because you've got a dirty mind and can only think of people's breasts all the time."

I touched them. They felt soft through the light material. "Come on, let's lie down again," I said, trying to sound enticing.

"Why? So we can screw?"

"Not necessarily. . . . I just thought we could lie together and . . ."

"—talk about astronomy?" Leda snapped. "All you want to do is get our clothes off and fuck."

"Don't *you* want to?" I said. "I thought you liked it too."

"I like it, but not all the time! Not when you've been acting like such a schmuck. All of a sudden after you've been insulting me for half an hour, just because you're horny I'm supposed to pull off my clothes and get in a romantic mood. Well, I'm not *like* that!"

I remembered how my father had said, "Don't be a

schmuck with women." I wondered if this was what he meant. "We could just lie here and talk," I said, stroking her shoulder and trying to sound sincere and soothing.

Leda lay down next to me. "What should we talk about—funeral homes?"

The trouble was I suddenly did feel incredibly horny. I don't know what it was, maybe that Leda is so pretty and that when she gets mad, she sounds so passionate and fiery. Maybe just the awkwardness of the dinner and relief it was over.

"You have an erection," Leda said, as though I might not be aware of that.

"I know," I said apologetically.

"So, let's just take our clothes off and get it over with," she said.

"I don't want to do it unless you're in the mood," I lied.

"It's better than arguing," Leda said.

That's true, actually. It's a lot better. In fact, I wished we had just done it right at the beginning and not gotten into that stupid argument about funeral homes and nuns and bras. In some way I felt sort of ashamed for having taken it out on Leda about feeling awkward during the dinner. I always feel especially that way when my brother is around. Maybe it's the age gap between us. I know that in his eyes I'm permanently about nine years old, trailing him around the house, overcome with joy if he'll play a game of checkers with me. And I kept wondering if Leda, if she had the choice, wouldn't prefer him. Knox knows how to handle women. He wouldn't have gotten into this stupid argument. Look how he calmed Angelica down.

Still, it was good. It's different each time, though. I guess in the beginning the sheer wonder and amazement of doing it is so incredible that you don't even think about any of the subtleties, about how the girl is reacting. I mean, you want her to be enjoying herself, but that's about it. You just assume she is unless she's wailing aloud in agony. But this time I had the feeling both of us were enjoying it physically, but somewhat apart in any other way. Maybe it just has to be like that if you do it often, but it wasn't the best feeling in the world.

When we were finished, Leda lay there quietly, not saying much. "I guess I better get home," she said. "I said I'd be back at six."

I wanted to change the mood of the afternoon, but I didn't know how. She started getting dressed. "Do you think that's what they've been doing?"

"Who?"

"Your brother and his—"

"Probably."

"I bet she's frigid," Leda said, fastening her skirt. "She probably lies there like a corpse." She laughed grimly. "Get it?"

"I doubt it," I said, ignoring her attempt at a joke.

"Why? Have you two made it together? Do you want to swap partners or something?"

"No," I said angrily. "Do you?"

"No!"

"Then, why'd you bring it up?"

"I didn't!" Leda said. "I said she was frigid and you said you knew she wasn't."

"All I meant," I said, "is that I doubt Knox would marry someone who didn't like sex."

"Oh, he'll probably cheat on her the first week they're married," Leda said.

"That's pretty cynical," I said, though actually I wasn't sure it was that far off the mark.

"Maybe. . . . He just seems the type. Listen, I'm sure he's a great guy, great in bed, anyway—"

"What makes you say that?"

"Well, you said he's had a million girls and he just, he has that manner. Ramon was a little like that."

"Like what?"

"Oh, Joel, come on! You know . . . sort of suave and come-hitherish. That way of leaning over and looking right at you when you say something, as though you were the most fascinating person that ever lived."

Actually, that's exactly what my brother is like. "I think they love each other," I said, for some reason.

"Sure," Leda said. "Just like us, right?"

I felt like she had stabbed me, that horrible combination of flipness and vulnerability, as though she were pulling two strings at once. "Yeah, like us," I said, trying to smile.

After Leda left, I just lay on my bed for about an hour. I felt about as depressed as I ever had. There's one peculiar thing about having sex with someone. It's that everything else you do with them is heightened. It's either much better or much worse than doing that same thing with someone else, like a friend. Like, some afternoons Leda and I have just sat around listening to records or we've taken a walk or something not at all unusual and it's been wonderful. But now our having argued made me feel a million times worse than if I'd argued with Berger, say. I've argued with Berger lots of times, we've had some big fights, but I've never felt afterward like life wasn't worth living. Don't worry. I wasn't about to slit my wrists. That was just the way I felt, like I was completely emptied out emotionally. I thought of that line in *The Joy of Sex*: "It can give us some of our best experiences and some of our worst." I think I'm beginning to know what they mean.

❧ 13 ❧

Angelica and Knox left on March first. They're getting married in June, probably in L.A., but that isn't definite yet. Mom and Dad seemed basically happy about the whole thing. "I think she'll make him a good wife," Dad said the day before they left. They were out seeing some friends of Knox's.

"Sweetie, that just sounds so horribly sexist," Mom said. "What *is* a good wife, for heaven's sake?"

"Well, of course, she has to earn at least fifty thousand a year," Dad said ironically, "be great in bed, a wonderful mother, have a superb net game at tennis, be able to prepare at least six gourmet dishes—"

"*You* are talking your way into a divorce," Mom said. But they were obviously kidding around.

I wondered, though. Angelica may make fifty thousand a

year, but I can't quite picture her doing all those other things Dad mentioned.

"Don't you want her to sew a fine seam," Mom said, kissing Dad on the neck, "and be able to strum gently on the zither in the evening, sing lieder?"

"You wouldn't let me finish," Dad said. "I was just getting started."

Mom went into the next room to do something. I went into my room to practice my guitar. I hadn't been doing it every day like I should, and you really do get rusty if you let even a couple of days go by. Your fingers get stiff or something. While I was playing, there was a knock at the door. "Yeah?" I said.

It was Dad.

"Joel?"

"What?"

Dad looked uncomfortable. "I don't mean to interfere in any way with your social life or whatever, but I just wondered, uh, what form of birth control do you favor?"

"I don't favor any method," I said, looking right at him.

Dad looked alarmed. "Does Leda favor any method?"

"She has a diaphragm," I said. "Does that set your mind at rest?"

"It does if she's using it," Dad said.

"She is."

Actually, that's more of an assumption on my part than an actual fact. Sometimes Leda will come over, saying she has it in already. I don't bother stopping and cross-examining her each time.

Before my brother left, he offered me some jackets he didn't wear that much anymore. We're about the same size now, though he's more muscular around the shoulders. "I don't wear jackets that much," I said. "But thanks."

"I thought maybe now that you have a girl—"

I didn't feel like talking about Leda with him. I was afraid he'd start making some dirty jokes. "Do you think you'll like being married?" I said.

Knox smiled. "Yeah . . . I'm ready, I mean, obviously you never know till you've tried it, but—"

"What made you pick her?" I asked. "I mean, she seems very nice, I just wondered."

"Well, obviously she's gorgeous," Knox said, "but that's not it, basically. It's just—she has a great mind. I know that's a cliché, but that girl has a mind like a steel trap. She came down once to my office and looked over my records, how I was billing patients, and in two hours she'd worked out a new system that was ten times more efficient. She's like Mom that way, not great at abstract reasoning, but she could run any business you name. I really admire that."

It didn't sound like the most romantic reason in the world to fall in love with someone and marry them, but who knows. She didn't seem that gorgeous to me, either. Pretty, but not gorgeous.

"Don't fuck up with Leda," he said, hanging the jackets in my closets.

"What do you mean?" My heart started thumping.

"Well, excuse the brotherly advice, but you acted pretty shitty to her that day she came over for dinner."

"Why'd she have to act like that?" I said, feeling annoyed all over again. "Singing that dopey song, babbling on like a fool—"

"Listen, do you love her?"

"Yeah."

"Show it, okay?"

I felt flustered and annoyed at the condescending tone he was using. "I do."

"I don't mean just in bed. I mean—"

"I get it," I said curtly.

"She's a real cutie," he repeated, grinning.

It's always a relief when my brother leaves. I hate to say

this, but I'm glad he lives in California. I think we would get along pretty badly if he lived in New York. Maybe this is paranoid of me, but I bet he'd make a pass at Leda if he was in the mood, whether he's engaged to Angelica or not. And the awful part is she might take him up on it. It's not going to happen, but the thought of it makes me nervous and mad at both of them.

Angelica gave me a big hug good-bye. She said I was just like the brother she'd always wished she had. She said she hoped I'd come out and visit them often and bring my girl friend with me. I said sure.

The week after they left Berger called me up on Sunday, sounding really manic. "Listen, you've got to come over here instantly," he said.

"It's five o'clock."

"I don't care. Get a cab and be here by ten past."

"Berg, I—"

"Can't talk on the phone. See you."

What was I supposed to do? I went over to his house. He took me straight into his room and closed the door. "She called!" he said. I've never seen Berger look that way, so excited and happy.

"What?" I said.

"She called!"

"Berg, what are you talking about? Who?"

"Who?" He looked at me like I was crazy. "The love of my life, you fool! The doctor, the lady doctor!"

"Oh." Berger put those signs up about two months ago and hadn't heard anything so I'd kind of forgotten about it. "What'd she say?"

Berger was smoking away furiously, lighting one cigarette after another. "Well, she said she'd seen the signs over a month ago, but she'd hesitated about getting in touch with me. She was afraid I might be, you know, kind of weird, the

Boston Strangler or something. She's in training to be a shrink, so that's her specialty. But she said she reread my note several times and she decided I definitely didn't have psychotic tendencies, that the feeling behind the note was sincere and touching and it was her moral responsibility to see me."

"So, when are you going to see her?"

"This Friday!" Berger said. "My God, I can't believe it. She's going to meet me!"

"Where?"

"Well, I guess she's still a little nervous that I might be, you know. . . . So, she wouldn't give me her phone number or tell me where she lived or worked. She said she'd meet me at a restaurant at Fifty-ninth and Third after work."

"It's a real date, then?"

Berger was grinning from ear to ear. "Something . . . I'm going to *see* her, Joel! God, you don't know. I was really beginning to give up hope. I was going to enter a monastery. I was going to pledge celibacy forever. And now—"

"But listen, even if she's willing to see you, it sounds more like . . . she feels sorry for you in a way. I doubt she's thinking of—" I wasn't trying to throw cold water on his plan, just be realistic.

"Look, it's a foot in the door, right? Once I get there, I will be so suave, so charming, so intelligent, so terrific in every way that she'll fall at my feet."

"Sure."

Berger looked at me suspiciously. "What's wrong with you? I thought you were in love."

"But Leda's my age. She—"

"So? You've really got hang-ups about age, you know that? What does it matter? It's maturity that counts."

I laughed.

"What're you laughing about?"

"Are you that mature?"

"Of course I am! . . . Hey, are you my friend or not? Sure I horse around a lot, but I'm *extremely* mature for my age."

"How old will you tell her you are?"

He looked thoughtful. "Well, it depends partly on how old she says *she* is. . . . I'll keep it within seven years. If she's twenty-seven, I'll say twenty."

"She'll never believe you're twenty."

"I thought of maybe—I've got to look perfect. Will you lend me one of those jackets your brother left you? I have to look sharp, but casual."

"I don't know if they'll fit you. He's pretty muscular."

"That's okay . . . I can look muscular if I put my mind to it." He crushed out his cigarette and opened the window to let the smoke out. It was really cold out. "Look, there's just one thing. I don't want my parents to know what's going on, for obvious reasons. So could I come over to your house and change there?"

"Sure . . . I'm seeing Leda at eight thirty, though."

"No problem . . . I told Ingrid I'd meet her at six thirty."

"Ingrid?"

"I knew she'd have a beautiful name," Berger said dreamily.

"I thought you said she had black hair. Ingrid sounds Scandinavian. Maybe that's not her real name."

"She wouldn't give me her real *last* name. . . . No, she's an Ingrid, all right. She looks like an Ingrid. Great cheekbones, icy blue eyes." As I was about to leave Berger hugged me. "I love you," he said passionately. "I love everybody. I love the whole damn world! I love—I even love Mr. Jazinski!"

Mr. Jazinski is our Phys. Ed. teacher who's always

humiliating Berger in class because he won't even swing when he's up at bat in softball. He just stands there, gazing off into space. "That's your one hundred tenth strikeout," he'll say. "Or is it one hundred twentieth?" "Who's counting?" Berger says. On the way home I thought about Berger's date. It's great he's so elated, but I really think he's setting himself up for a fall. How can he imagine that this doctor is going to believe he's twenty? Someone would believe that about me quicker than they'd believe that about him. It's not just looks, and Berger isn't that tall. It's personality. If you put my brother at one end of the spectrum, as far as suaveness with women and life in general goes, Berger would be way *way* down at the other end. Don't get me wrong. He's my best friend, but he's not what people would call "mature." Manic maybe. Maybe she'll take him on as a patient.

I don't totally believe this, but I also started thinking how maybe the mood Berger's in now, before he's really met her or gotten to know her, is the best. You can imagine anything, you can make the person into anything in your mind. Reality is a little more tricky.

Friday night Berger came over at five thirty. He didn't look that good, sort of anxious and wrought up. "What'd you do to your hair?" I said.

He cringed. "Was that stupid? I dyed it just a little on the sides, so it would look like I was going gray early."

"It looks more like you walked under a ladder with a pot of gray paint on it."

"Listen, do me a favor, just tell me good things tonight, okay? Like, I look great, it's all going to work out, she's going to love me."

I showed him Knox's jackets. "Which one do you like best?"

Berger took them all out and tried them on one by one. Frankly, none of them looked that great. Knox has longer arms than Berger and they all hung down over the shoulders. Berger looked at himself in the mirror. "Maybe the tweedy one with the suede patches. I look kind of . . . academic, intellectual. What do you think?"

"It doesn't go that well with your shirt."

"Can you lend me a shirt? The tweed is definitely it. She's got to be smart, right? A doctor and all . . . I don't want to look schlumpy."

"Right."

I gave him a shirt and he exchanged it for the one he had on. "So, what do you think?" he said, standing up straight, which he never does normally.

"Terrific," I said, trying hard to sound sincere.

"How old? Just roughly."

I sighed. "Do you want the truth?"

"No. Forget the truth."

"If she's *very* nearsighted, maybe twenty. Otherwise, maybe nineteen or eighteen."

Berger sat down. He looked morose. "I want her to love me!" he said.

"She can't love you on a first date."

"Sure, she can. . . . Haven't you ever seen those movies when two people take one look at each other and whammo!"

"Yeah, but you already did look at each other."

"But that was under strange circumstances. Tonight there'll be candlelight. I'll ply her with strong drinks. I'll be witty. I'll gaze deeply into her eyes. . . ."

"Good luck," I said.

He turned to go, then turned back. "Should I smoke? If I don't, I may start chewing on the tablecloth. On the other hand, if she's a doctor, she may think it's unhealthy."

"Don't chain-smoke. But maybe a few—"

"Yeah, right . . . I mean, she has to know the real me.

And all creative, interesting people have addictions of one kind or another. Look, I've heard lots of doctors are stoned all the time. . . Not her, but it's not uncommon." He grinned. "See you."

❧ 14 ❧

If Berger has a patron saint, I hope she's around tonight. I think he's going to need all the help he can get. But then, look at Leda and me. I still don't exactly know why she fell for me. It's not like she's desperate, never met other guys. Maybe it is kind of mysterious.

I'd told Leda I'd meet her at this apartment near hers where she was baby-sitting. She said the couple had a baby who went to bed at seven so it would be basically like a real date for us.

When she let me in, she said, "Hi," in a whisper. "I just put him in," she explained, still whispering. "He seemed to want to stay up and play."

Leda was wearing plain jeans and a T-shirt. Her feet were bare. She doesn't like wearing shoes indoors, she says.

There was an interesting smell in the air, like mashed potatoes. I sniffed inquiringly.

"Let's go in the kitchen," she said. She closed the door to the kitchen and looked at the wall clock. "It said it's got to come out in fifty minutes," she said.

"What?"

"I'm making this potato bread. . . . Danny got the recipe from her aunt. It's terrific. You can make it with potato flakes, but I used real ones. Mrs. Balaban said it was okay if I cooked it here. So I brought the batter over." She smiled. "Isn't it a great smell?"

"Yeah," I said. It was.

"I love fresh bread," Leda said. "So, listen, should we watch TV, or what? We can do anything, as long as I remember to take it out at nine."

I laughed. "Anything?"

"Well, maybe not anything. . . . I mean, you know the baby might wake up or they could come home early."

"Sure," I said. "Let's watch TV, then. Is anything good on?"

We went into the living room and settled down on the couch in front of the TV. Leda snuggled up against me. I always feel there's something slightly hypocritical going on between us and I don't know if it's my fault or what. It's like there are four of us. First, just Leda and me, two regular people who sometimes get along and sometimes don't, the way Berger and I sometimes get along and sometimes don't. But then there are our bodies, which basically just want to fuck. I hate to put it that crudely, but it's true. Leda once said she hated some book she read where a man cheated on his wife or girl friend and said, as an excuse, "It wasn't me, it was him," meaning his cock. I admit that's kind of a dodge, but I also know what he means. I can feel really pissed off at Leda, at the way she's acting or whatever or even be interested in something she's saying, but there's

137

also part of me that's thinking, *When are we going to get around to doing it?* Maybe girls aren't as much like that. I don't know. I try not to show it. I mean, if she doesn't seem in the mood, I don't push it, but that doesn't mean I'm not thinking about it.

So there we were, watching this dumb TV movie and frankly I wasn't hearing more than about a third of the dialogue. I was just aware of Leda's body against mine, hoping she might suddenly turn around and start kissing me and get carried away, even forget about that damn potato bread. She was acting affectionate and friendly, but not that sexy, so far, so I didn't get my hopes up.

"Do you think she's pretty?" she said during a commercial break.

"Who?" I said.

"Valerie Bertinelli."

"Who's she?"

"Joel! She's the star of the movie!"

"Oh . . . you mean, the dark-haired one?"

"No, I mean the dog! . . . Who did you *think* I meant?"

"I guess I haven't been concentrating all that much," I admitted.

"Why not?"

I swallowed. "It's sort of hard for me to concentrate with you around."

"All you think about is sex," Leda said angrily.

"No," I protested. "It's just . . . Listen, don't you think about it too?"

"Sure, some of the time. Not *all* the time!"

"But I mean, say, like now, what if it weren't for the potato bread and the baby and the fact that the whatever their name is might come back, would you want to—"

Leda leaped up. "Oh, God, thanks for reminding me! It's time to take it out." She rushed into the kitchen to rescue

138

the potato bread. We waited while it cooled off. "Do you want to see the baby?" Leda said.

"Sure, I guess," I said. To me most babies look alike, but I went into the baby's bedroom with her to look at him. He was lying in his crib, on his back, sleeping. It's funny the way babies lie like dogs almost, their hands on either side, like they were waiting for someone to rub their bellies. "Isn't he cute?" Leda whispered.

"Yeah," I whispered back.

"He's adopted," she said when we were back in the kitchen. "They tried to have one of their own, you know, the regular way, but they couldn't, so they flew all the way to Lebanon to get him." She sliced a piece of bread off. "I think we can eat it now. It's still warm." She buttered two pieces and we each had one. I have to admit, it was great; the best bread I ever tasted.

"I'm going to save some for the Balabans," Leda said, "and the rest I'll take home. You can take some too, Joel. Do you want to? For breakfast?"

"Sure," I said.

We went back into the living room and sat down where we'd been before, on the couch. The movie was over so we didn't have to turn the TV set on again. "Do you see what I mean, though?" I said. This is a habit of mine which may not always be so good. When I get started in a conversation, I hate to stop till I feel I understand everything.

"What?" Leda said. She looked distracted.

"About it being hard for me to concentrate with you around?"

"Yeah, I guess it's sort of flattering, in a way," she said, frowning and twisting her hair around her finger. "I'm not always in the mood, that's all. . . . Like, sometimes I'm worried about something which has nothing to do with you. Doesn't that ever happen to you?"

139

"Are you worried about something tonight?" I asked. She certainly looked that way.

She sighed. "Oh, kind of. . . . It's probably silly, but—"

"What?"

Leda made a face. "My period's late," she said. Before I could say anything, she said, "Listen, don't panic or anything. It's been late before. In fact, sometimes I skip a month. If we weren't, you know, doing anything, I wouldn't even worry."

"I thought you always used a diaphragm," I said, beginning to feel nervous myself.

"Usually," she said. "But I don't know, lots of things can happen. It might not be in the right place."

"What do you mean usually?"

"I mean, like usually I brush my teeth at night," Leda said sarcastically, "but I don't brush them every single night of my life! Sometimes I'm too tired, sometimes I forget."

"Did you ever forget to put it in?" I was going from nervous to panicked very quickly.

"Just a couple of times," Leda said. "I mean, like, remember the time we were studying at your house and your parents called and said they wouldn't be home for dinner? Well, I didn't go over expecting us to do anything, so I left it at home."

"Oh."

"Look, don't start worrying," Leda said, touching my shoulder. "I'm sure it's going to be okay. I wasn't even going to mention it. It's just you brought up why I don't always feel like—"

"No, I'm glad you told me," I said, not sure if I was or not.

Leda moved over and sat on my lap. She put her arms around me. "Kiss me, okay?" she said.

We started kissing, for some reason very slowly, which

got me more excited than usual, even. Leda slipped her hand under my shirt and started caressing my back all around, down to where my jeans began. I wasn't sure exactly what was going on. She was certainly acting very passionate for someone who wasn't in the mood. I looked at her in the half darkness, trying to figure out what was going on.

"I'd feel funny if we did it in their bedroom," Leda said softly. "They might be able to tell."

"Where should we go then?" I was having trouble talking.

"They have this maid's room. It's kind of messy, but there's a studio bed in it. Is that okay?"

I decided not to try and figure out the sequence of the evening. It wasn't like I had been saying I was very fussy about where we did it! The maid's room was small, a bike leaning against one wall, a few cartons of books in the corner. It smelled stuffy, like it wasn't used much for anything. We did it quickly. I guess I was scared they might come home unexpectedly and also not sure which way Leda's mood would swing the next moment. Suddenly she seemed so passionate! I had no idea why. She gripped my shoulders so hard I was afraid she'd tear the skin. As she came, she cried out, "Joel!" almost as though she were being run over or were in pain.

Afterward we got back into our clothes and lay there with our arms around each other. She still seemed in an affectionate mood. Snuggling against me, she kissed my collarbone and bit my earlobe lightly, like a kitten.

Probably this was a stupid thing to say, but I said, "Lee, are you, uh, wearing it now?"

"What?"

"Your diaphragm."

"Yeah! . . . Do you want me to take it out so you can examine it?"

"No, I just—"

"Look, what's done is done. If I'm pregnant, I'm pregnant."

Pregnant is a strange word. It hung there in the air. Everything about the evening, in fact, began seeming strange to me, even though I didn't think Leda had planned it that way—the moment when we looked in on the baby, the potato bread, her going back and forth about sex. Maybe she was feeling mixed up about what she wanted too. I certainly was.

She must have sensed some of my anxiety because she said, "What are you worried about? We don't have to get married or anything. I'll just get rid of it. I don't care!" She laughed. "Or maybe I'll have it and give it to the Balabans. They really want a baby sister for Keith."

"Do you really think you're pregnant?" I asked. The way she kept going back and forth between joking around about it and sounding scared puzzled me.

"I don't know." She sighed. "I guess pregnancy is the punishment for sex," she said. "Sex is the crime and pregnancy is the punishment . . . for women."

"I don't think it's a crime," I said.

"For men it's not," Leda said. She sounded angry. "It's so unfair!"

We lay there together a long time. I feel so many different things about Leda, sometimes all in the space of one evening, that it confuses me. And it was the same about this. Part of me in some crazy way felt proud that I could be the father of a baby. Part of me felt really angry that she was careless enough not to use the diaphragm every time. She could have told me! I have some condoms. I could have used those. I don't think she was trying to trap me. Knowing her personality, I think it's more that she's like Berger, sort of impulsive, giving in to the mood of the moment, not always that organized.

142

"I feel angry at myself too," she said. "I should have been careful."

"What do you mean, at yourself too? Who else are you angry at?"

"You," she blurted out.

"Thanks."

"I just mean it's not totally your fault."

"I guess I don't see how it's my fault at all."

"Well, if you're so interested in doing it, you could have, like, gotten condoms so it wasn't always my responsibility."

"I *do* have them."

"Then, why didn't you tell me?"

"Because you said you had a diaphragm! . . . And I *assumed* you were using it."

"Don't you ever forget anything?"

"Yeah, sometimes, but I don't think with something that important, I'd—"

"Okay, so you're perfect! It's all my fault! I'm just an irresponsible dope."

"I didn't *say* it was your fault. . . . We just should have talked about it, maybe."

"But when you're in a sexy mood, you don't seem to *want* to talk," she said dolefully. "It's like I'm not there."

I felt really shitty. "Look, I don't know, Lee. . . . Maybe you're right. Anyway, why worry about it now if it might not even be necessary?"

"True," Leda said.

There was a silence.

Maybe I should've shut up, but I said instead, "I can't always figure out what you're feeling. Like tonight. First you said you weren't in the mood, then suddenly it seemed like you were—"

"I thought you'd be mad if we didn't."

"I wouldn't have been mad. I just would've been disappointed."

"Well, whatever. I didn't want you to be disappointed."

"Didn't you feel like doing it too?" I persisted.

"Sure." Leda smiled mischievously. "You look so sexy when you get that funny, glazed expression, like when you didn't even know who Valerie Bertinelli was."

"Homemade potato bread really turns me on."

"Really?" She looked pleased. "It was good, wasn't it? I think I'm a good cook."

"You're a good everything," I said, loving her again.

The rest of the evening was okay. It wasn't like anything had been settled, but I still felt better. But for the first time, going home, I was really glad Leda didn't go to my school. In fact, I was glad there weren't any girls in my class. I didn't want to have to spend all week thinking about this, worrying about it. In some ways school was a relief. I don't really give a damn about French verbs or the fall of Rome, but it's great sometimes to have to concentrate on something that has no personal connection with your life.

❧ 15 ❧

I tend to get to school early, at least half an hour before classes start. I just like having that amount of time to get my thoughts organized. Berger's the opposite. He usually zooms in about one second before the bell rings. But that Monday he came half an hour early too. I had completely forgotten about his date with the lady doctor, what with worrying about Leda. I remembered when I saw him. "So, how'd it go?" I asked.

He grinned from ear to ear. "Fantastic!"

"Was she as good as you remembered?"

"Better . . . God, am I glad I didn't know how terrific she really is, because I never would've put up that note. I would've been too scared."

"How old did you tell her you were?"

"Almost nineteen. . . . She's twenty-four."

"Did she seem to mind?"

"I don't think so. . . . I mean, I did lie quite a bit. Not lie—well, exaggerate, concoct, whatever."

"What about?"

"I told her . . ." He looked sheepish. ". . . Well, that I'd dropped out of college to try my hand at acting, that I was studying at the Actors Studio."

"And she bought that?"

"Yeah, she said her kid brother was really interested in acting too and that maybe when he came to New York, we could see some plays together. She said she really admired creative people, but that she didn't think *she* was creative, but she thought if she was a shrink, she'd like treating creative people who had, like, blocks or neuroses about their work. . . . I said I could be her first patient."

"So, what's going to happen. . . . Will you see her again?"

"Yeah! . . . Joel, listen, I was great! I was *so* great! I wish I could have videotaped the whole thing because you'll never believe it. I didn't come on really strong. I acted subdued, kind of quiet. She said she'd worried about me after that night, how I was, if my leg was healing. I said I had lived in New York all my life and that it was really unusual to find someone that compassionate. She said that was why she'd become a doctor, that caring for people really turned her on. She didn't say 'turned her on,' but that was the idea. She said one thing she didn't like about New York was that people here don't seem that caring, they just rush around, only thinking about themselves. She's from some town in Oregon or something that only has three hundred people where, if you have a cold, the postman comes out in the driving rain to bring you a letter, even if it's just from your aunt or grandmother or something."

"Doesn't she have a boyfriend, though?" I hated to be

the cold voice of reason, but I felt it would be better for Berger to face reality now than later.

"No! Listen, this is what's so great! We were talking about what I said, how New York is such an awful place, so cold and ruthless and stuff. I was just letting her talk, agreeing with everything. I mean, Christ, if she'd said the moon was made of green cheese, I'd have agreed. Anyway, when she was telling me about her hometown—boy, it sounds like a real disaster area!—she said how what she missed here were human connections. She said how at the hospital all the doctors seemed so cold and uninterested in anything except advancing their own careers. Then she began telling me about how all these middle-aged professors she has, married ones, keep making passes at her. 'I find that so distasteful,' she said. Don't you love that? You should have seen her face! You know, kind of perplexed, like here are all these really gross married guys coming on to her and she says, 'I find that sort of thing so distasteful, don't you?' "

I laughed. "What'd you say?"

"I said I thought it was disgusting, horrible, that guys like that ought to be put in jail, that people who didn't regard marriage as a holy sacrament were sick, sick people."

"Berg, don't you think that's a little—"

"Listen, this is what's weird. When I was talking to her, I believed every word. I would have gone out and personally shot or strangled *all* of those guys. One of them threatened not to give her a recommendation unless she put out for him! I wanted the whole restaurant to go up in flames! I kept having these fantasies of it being some kind of firetrap and we'd be stuck, unable to get out, and I'd have to gather her up in my arms, charge through columns of flame and smoke." He stood there, looking dazed.

"So what was the conclusion? Are you going to see her again?"

"She gave me her address and her phone number, her number at work. She said if I ever felt lonely or just wanted to talk, I should call her, no matter what time of day or night. 'I think we could really help each other,' she said. 'It may sound funny, but psychiatrists need someone to talk to too.'" Berger sighed. "I said she should call *me* at any hour of day or night."

"What if your parents answer?"

"I told her I was living at home to save money for my acting lessons. She said she understood that, that she had a friend who was doing the same thing."

Maybe I'm being overly suspicious. It just seems to me something's got to not work in this. It sounds too cockeyed. "So, you're just going to be friends?"

"We'll be whatever she wants us to be," Berger said intensely. "Look, Joel, she likes me, she wants to talk to me, to be with me."

"I thought you wanted more than that. I thought you were in love with her."

"I'd rather sit there listening to her talk about the postman in her hometown than screw anyone you can name. I mean *anyone*."

"Bo Derek? Cheryl Ladd?"

"Anyone!" he shouted.

The bell rang.

Berger was really in a bad way. All day he hardly seemed there in classes when the teachers called on him. The worst was in Gym, which is our last class. We were playing basketball, which is not one of Berger's strong points, not that any sport is. One thing I find about sports that I like is that concentrating on it kind of blanks your mind out in a good way. Like, I could've spent all day worrying about Leda and whether or not she was pregnant, but I did the opposite. I concentrated on every subject, even the dumb ones, and when we played basketball, I played like my life depended on it. Berger tossed the ball to me. That would've been okay, except we were on opposite teams. Mr. Jazinski blew his whistle.

"Uh . . . Wolfson?" Mr. Jazinski said. "Do you think you could explain your strategy in that particular move?"

Berger just looked at him. "What's to explain?"

"Well, it seemed like a peculiar move, given that Davis is on the opposite team."

Berger shrugged.

"That's an eloquent shrug, Wolfson. . . . Does it signify anything special?"

"Not especially." I could tell Berger was getting angry.

"Well, maybe you could explain to all of us why, in every game we play, you seem unable to concentrate on *any* of the rules, to give even lip service to the most bottom level of sportsmanship, are constantly and consistently arrogant *and* thoroughly incompetent."

"Sure, I'll tell you why," Berger said nervously but loudly. "It's because I think sports are dumb."

"Dumb? Is there any reason for that? Any 'experience' that has driven you to that conclusion?"

"Yeah, actually it's that every guy I've ever known who liked sports was a total asshole," Berger said, "and every coach I've ever had was like you, Mr. Jazinski, a grade Z jerk and a total Neanderthal. That's why!"

Mr. Jazinski had turned a shade of purplish red. "You're aware, Wolfson, that no one has ever graduated this school without passing physical education?"

"Oh, fuck off, Mr, Jazinski," Berger said and walked off the court.

There were two minutes of total silence. Then Mr. Jazinski looked out at all of us. My heart was thumping so loudly that I was afraid everyone could hear it. I was really scared. "I'd like to take advantage of Mr. Wolfson's tantrum," Mr. Jazinski said. "I think it should give us all food for thought." You could tell he was ready to explode, but he talked in this very calm, methodical way. "You see, life is full of losers, guys who, for one reason or another, can't make it. They can't make it in sports, they can't make it in their jobs, they can't make it in their personal lives. Why? Okay, some of these guys may come from rotten homes, maybe it's genetic in some cases, but the fact is most of them don't even bother. Most of them are rotten kids that never grew up and never even tried. And you know where these guys end up? They end up sleeping on park benches, they end up assassinating our president, they end up as worthless punks! . . . I don't care if all of you are great at basketball. Maybe you're not. But if you want to end up like Wolfson, that's your problem. And it's your choice, okay?"

It was the end of the class. No one said anything. I went into the locker room to change. Berger wasn't there. Some of the guys started talking about it a little. I think most of them think Jazinski's pretty much of a jerk, but still, it wasn't the kind of confrontation that happens every day. Is this what being in love does to you? I wondered what the lady doctor from Oregon would have said if she'd seen Berger today. And yet, in a crazy way, I admire Berg for doing it. It was stupid. Like, he could really not graduate, but I admire it anyway.

When I got home, Leda called. She sounded so peppy and friendly, I was sure she'd gotten her period. I felt really relieved. "Listen, I'm sorry I was in kind of a funny mood Friday," she said.

"Oh, that's okay," I said magnanimously.

"It's just my personality," she said. "I tend to worry a lot about things even when, like you said, it might not even be necessary."

150

There was a moment of silence. "Did you, uh, get it, your period, I mean?"

"Uh uh. . . . But you know, I decided you were right, Joel. . . . Like, I was going to rush out and get one of those pregnancy tests where you do it at home, but then I remembered the exact same thing happened to me before."

"You got pregnant?"

"No! I missed my period. See, my period was due once on June sixth and I didn't get it till August sixth! I just completely skipped one whole month! Our teacher said the body does that. If the body is worried, it just goes on strike, sort of, that's what she said. . . . So I'm going to wait till April ninth since that's two months after I got it last time."

April ninth happens to be just before my birthday. "Why not take the test now?" I said. "Then you'd know."

"Yeah, but I don't know, sometimes it's not reliable and then you keep taking it and sometimes it says you're pregnant and sometimes not. . . . And the thing is, I just know I'm going to get it on April ninth. I just have that feeling."

Somehow the logic behind Leda's decision didn't seem that ironclad to me. But our English teacher always says when you read a novel, you have to read between the lines, not just the plot but what the book is trying to say, the subtext. It seemed to me what Leda was trying to say was she wanted an extra month of not worrying, of just feeling free. And I wanted that too. It's just that, if it was me that might've been pregnant I'd have taken the test. I'd rather know for sure one way or the other.

The irony is that, ever since Angelica left, all my mother talks about is babies. She's really looking forward to having a grandchild. She said she and Angelica had this talk, while they were here, and Angelica said her first "task" of married life will be to "leave no stone unturned" in getting pregnant. I never thought it was a matter of turning or unturning stones, but anyhow, I guess that's a euphemism for fucking all day long till they hit it. I made some jocular remark to that effect and Mom turned on me indignantly.

"Joel, you may not be able to sympathize with this, but it's very difficult for many women to get pregnant. I tried for five straight *years* with you, I mean Frank and I. . . . There are so many complexities and it can be heartbreaking! You see women everywhere with babies, babies they don't want or need, and you feel so excluded, so terrible. Now I'm not saying that will happen with Angelica, but it's nothing to joke about."

"Sure." I wondered what Mom would say if I told her that there was a good chance she was a potential grandmother right this second. Maybe there was something revealing or peculiar in my expression because Mom said in a flustered way, "Are you and Leda . . . I don't mean to pry, but—"

"Yeah," I said. "We are."

"And does she, is there—"

"She has a diaphragm." I figured it was easier finishing my mother's sentences than watching her agonize through them.

"Diaphragms are such ghastly things!" my mother exclaimed. "Why doesn't she go on the Pill?"

"I think she thinks it's dangerous."

"Oh, that's all such nonsense," Mom said vehemently. "They make up all those stories just to scare people. They want women to get pregnant, that's all there is to it. They're just afraid if they don't sit home having babies they'll take jobs away from men. And they're right! They will! Because they're better and they *should* have those jobs!"

Did I mention that my mother is a feminist? It's something that's sneaked up on her, but if you press the right button, or the wrong one, she can go off like a lighted firecracker. When she does, my father just sits there smiling ironically. I guess he's learned not to interfere, though sometimes he blows up and says she's exaggerating, like when she says that what men have done to women is worse than what the Nazis did to the Jews.

I've never, frankly, given any thought to babies. I know they exist and that everyone was one once, but that's about it. I guess I figured at some point in my life, when I was thirty or so, maybe I'd have a wife and a kid, but it isn't something I've ever planned out. Now, wherever I go, there seem to be babies all over the place. Or maybe they were always there and I didn't notice them.

Over the weekend, for instance, Leda said I should meet her in this playground near her house because she was taking the Balaban baby out to the park. It was a gorgeous day. It's just March, but it was around seventy degrees. You didn't even need a coat. Suddenly I felt glad that Leda had decided to take the extra month and not find out. She looked so pretty and bouncy, pushing the baby in the swing, and I started thinking how we'd have a whole month of having fun together, the way it was in the beginning.

All over the playground there were babies. Maybe because it was a weekend, a lot of them were with their fathers. Leda put Keith in one of those swings that has a bar in front. I think this baby is in love with Leda. You should have seen him in the swing. She would take his feet and push them so he could watch her while he swung. Some parents were pushing their babies from the back. He was going pretty high and every time he came down and she grabbed his feet, he let out a shriek of pleasure, almost a scream. He was watching her every second.

The man next to us looked pretty young, maybe in his twenties. He looked a little like our English teacher, Mr. DeLillo, just in that he had a big nose and shaggy blond hair. His baby was a girl and she was hardly swinging at all, more just sitting there, looking up at him and smiling. Her nose was running, but she didn't seem to notice. He smiled at her. Then to me he said, "I don't like to push her too high. I'm scared she'll fall out."

Evidently Leda wasn't scared of that at all. Keith was swinging about as high as the swing could go without making a complete circle in the air.

"Is that your baby?" he asked me.

"No, it's . . . my girl friend's baby-sitting."

"I thought you both looked a little young . . . though my wife was eighteen when we got married, I was twenty. We didn't have a cent, our parents both disowned us, but we figured what the hell."

I would have liked to ask him if he regretted it. He seemed like a fairly relaxed, genial person who would accept whatever happened to him.

"I would have liked a boy," he said, glancing at Keith, "but fate dictates."

Just then a woman, I guess his wife, came over. She had a pair of twins, one holding on to each hand. They were girls, around four or five. One was sucking a lollipop. "I want to swing!" one of them said.

"Give me the baby," she said to the man. "I'm going to take her back."

The man lifted the baby out of the swing. She'd fallen asleep and just slumped into the woman's arms. Then he lifted both twins, one after the other, over the fence. "These are baby swings," the one with the lollipop said contemptuously. "We want the *big* swings." They went down to the other end.

"See you," the man said, following them.

Leda was taking Keith out of the swing. "I guess we better bring him back," she said. She put him in his stroller. "Who was that man?" she said.

"Just someone who comes here, I guess."

"I like it when fathers come," Leda said. "Don't you?"

154

"Sure," I said.

"Danny's brother has a baby and he never once in his whole *life* changed her diaper or took her to the park!" Leda said. "Can you imagine! He, like, prides himself on *not* knowing how to change a diaper. If I was married to someone like that, I'd kill them!"

Upstairs Mrs. Balaban paid Leda for the baby-sitting. "I think he's ready for his nap," Leda said. She bent down and kissed the baby good-bye. She kissed his cheeks and the tip of his nose and both his ears. He held out his arms to her. "I've got to go, Keith," she said apologetically.

All of a sudden the baby started to scream, and I mean really scream. His mother tried to quiet him down, saying, "Leda will come back, sweetie. Don't worry. She'll come visit us soon."

I never realized babies had such strong feelings. I knew they cried if they were hungry or wanted you to change their diapers, but it was clear this kid just *wanted* Leda. He didn't want his mother or anything else. It was almost like a sexual thing. It's lucky babies can't have heart attacks because he was screaming so loud that he looked like he might have one. His face turned bright red. I wonder what it would be like if every time I wanted Leda, I acted like that. I guess you learn at some point that no matter how much you want something, you have to figure out more subtle ways to get it.

Leda was quiet while we walked outside the building. "I like him," she said finally. "He's a nice baby." She looked at me. "Don't you think so?"

"Sure," I said, just to be agreeable. "He seems nice."

❧ 16 ❧

We got a letter from my brother saying he and Angelica are going to be married in April, April eighteenth, instead of in June. It seems Angelica's parents were married on April eighteenth and they've been married twenty-five years and her sister got married on April eighteenth, so it's sort of a family tradition. It's convenient since I have spring vacation that week. All of us are going to fly out and stay at my brother's house in L.A. He has this really big house, even though he lives by himself; it has about three bedrooms and a big basement where he records songs he makes up.

Leda came for dinner the night the letter from my brother arrived. My parents have been on this big kick of how I go to Leda's house too much and they're afraid Leda's parents won't think they're "hospitable." In fact, my mother even called Leda's mother up and they're going to meet for a drink. It makes me slightly nervous, though I don't know why. None of them know about the fact that Leda might be pregnant so there's no reason the evening should have any heavy overtones, but sometimes I wish my mother wasn't that friendly.

"April's a nice time for a wedding," my father said. "We got married in April, Nan, remember?"

"Of course I remember!" my mother said. "How could I not remember? What anniversary is it for us this April?"

"Let's see," my father said. "Well, I'm fifty-four and we did the ignoble deed when I was twenty-two, so . . . thirty-two."

"I don't think that counts," my mother said. "It doesn't count till you get to fifty."

"Doesn't count?" my father said, looking horrified. "Thirty-two years? We don't even get part credit?"

Mom laughed. "No, I just mean, in terms of . . . you know, like on those little calendars. Fifty is gold, but till then it's just things like desk sets."

"I've always wanted a desk set," my father said.

"*My* parents have been married thirty-five years," Leda said.

"Really?" my mother said. "Do you have any older brothers and sisters?"

"No, they just . . . My mother wanted to keep on with her acting. . . . And they traveled a lot."

"I wonder why Knox switched it to April," my mother said, frowning.

"Because of her parents," I reminded her.

"Do you think that's the real reason?"

I shrugged. I reached over for the margarine, which was down at the other end of the table.

"What do you think the real reason is?" Leda asked.

"Well, this is silly probably," my mother said, "but it

157

just crossed my mind. . . . I wonder if they have to get married."

There was a pause.

"You mean, she's knocked up?" my father said, helping himself to more salad.

"Frank, what an expression! I just meant . . . Oh, I suppose it doesn't matter anyway."

"You'll be that much closer to a grandchild," my father said.

"True. . . . And they *were* going to get married anyway. It's just . . . I think people who look back and know they had to, well, there's always that feeling of being trapped in some way."

"Sweetie, you're concocting worries out of thin air," Dad said.

"I guess I am," my mother agreed.

"I'm going to do it like my mother," Leda said suddenly. "I'm not going to have a baby till I'm thirty. Because I think otherwise you don't have a chance to . . . do things."

"That's very sensible," my mother said. "Thirty seems a perfect age to me."

My parents went out at around eight. Leda and I were in my room. We were just listening to this terrific Jimi Hendrix record, my favorite one, when my mother knocked on my door and called, "See you later!" I guess they want to "respect my privacy." But I'd never in a million years do it with my parents in the house, never.

"Do you think they suspect anything?" Leda asked. She was sitting on the bed, leaning against the wall, cross-legged.

I shook my head.

"I felt funny when they, you know, began talking about people being trapped . . ."

"Yeah, I could tell," I said.

She frowned. "Did I look funny?"

"Not funny, just . . ."

"People always talk about how the guy is trapped!" Leda burst out. "But how about the girl?"

"They didn't say," I said. "You're just being hypersensitive."

Leda flushed. "Well, it's *my* body!" she said.

"Sure," I said nervously. Leda has such a wonderful body! It's a pity that it's partly because it's wonderful that we might be in trouble. I was afraid she might be about to explode, but she reached up and took my hand.

"Come sit down," she said, smiling. "They're gone."

I sat down beside her, putting my arms around her. I feel nervous with Leda these days. I'm afraid if I make anything like a pass at her, she'll get mad and say all I think about is sex, but if I don't, she might wonder if I don't like her that much. I kissed her lightly, to test the water as it were, and she kissed me back. Then she started taking off her clothes! For a second I just sat there hesitantly. Leda looked at me. "Don't you want to?" she asked.

"Sure," I said, starting to take my shirt off.

"Don't do me any favors!" she snapped.

"It's just . . . I'm afraid if we do it, if I say I want to, you'll think that's all I'm interested in."

"No, I don't think that." She smiled mischievously. "I know you basically love me for my wonderful creative mind and my sardonic wit. You just put up with my body because you don't want to hurt my feelings."

All my clothes were off. In that state it's hard to conceal what you're feeling. I lay down next to her and we began kissing and caressing each other. Leda was lying on top of me. Her body's shorter than mine, so her toes only come up to my legs, but it was terrific feeling all of her flat against me. "Should we do it this way?" she whispered. We never had.

"Sure," I said.

"They say it's better for the woman this way," Leda said. "You can, like, move around more."

It seems to me more or less any way is basically wonderful. I watched as Leda took my cock and fitted it inside her. "Is that okay?" she asked anxiously. "Does it feel okay?"

"It feels great," I said, closing my eyes. Leda has a great bottom. It's round and smooth and terrific to feel. Lying on my back that way, I could run my hands all over it, which it's hard to do the other way when I'm on top. All her breasts were hanging almost right in my face. Her nipples touched the tip of my nose, like soft flower petals. She moved back and forth slowly. I opened my eyes one second. Leda's eyes were closed too. She looked so beautiful that way, her hair falling into her face, her mouth slightly open. I'd been trying not to get too excited, but when I closed my eyes again, she made a sudden move, began going faster and I couldn't hold back. I gripped ahold of her and came, shooting up into her in short, sudden thrusts. Leda cried out and then collapsed on top of me, her hair falling into my face. We lay like that for several minutes. Then I withdrew and she lay beside me. She didn't nestle against me the way she sometimes does.

"Maybe it would be better if we didn't have bodies," Leda said. She sounded far off, not hostile, but not warm and gooey the way she usually does.

I looked over at her, not sure if she meant that.

"No, I mean . . . Like, do you think we'd be friends if it weren't for—"

"Sure," I said, more to reassure her than because I really thought so.

"I feel like we are and we're not," she said. "We're close about a lot of things, but it's not like with me and Danny, where we tell each other everything, we're completely open. I'm not sure you tell me everything you feel."

160

"I don't tell anyone else more than I tell you," I said. Which is true.

"That's not the same thing."

"Well." I felt hurt, though, because I feel we are close, even if it's in a different way than I'm friendly with Berger. "Uh, Lee, are you wearing your diaphragm?"

"What does it matter?"

"I thought you thought you *weren't* pregnant."

"I don't *think* I am. . . . But I *could* be. . . . Yeah, I'm wearing it. Does that set your mind at rest?"

"Yeah."

"Listen, you have nothing to worry about either way," Leda said. "We're not going to have a shotgun wedding, even if I am. I'll just have an abortion, that's all. . . . God, don't you hate those books for teen-agers where they *have* to get married and she drops out of school and they live over a garage and he works in some used car lot. And there's always some scene where some girl who had an abortion comes to visit and she's gone insane and becomes a Bowery bum, just in case you didn't get the point."

"I never read a book like that," I said.

"You're lucky. . . . Every other book I've read since I was *ten* is like that. The girl's a moron, the guy's a moron, they never heard of birth control. What I love are the scenes where the father takes the guy aside and says, 'Son, if you marry Betsy, you'll have to give up your football scholarship to Oklahoma State.' They're *always* going to some godforsaken place like Oklahoma State! And the guy says, 'But, Dad, I love her!' . . . And then there's a scene where the mother says, 'Dear, you haven't let him take advantage of you? You know what boys are like.' Quote unquote. . . . God, I think writers must be really dumb! Or else they're living in the Stone Age."

I really hope Leda isn't pregnant. I know abortions are legal and supposedly safe, but I still don't like the idea of it.

Leda was staring at me intensely. "I mean, at least we love each other!" she said. "We're not just two horny jerks who jumped into bed because we couldn't think of anything better to do."

"I love you a lot," I said. After a second I added, "You look glowing." I put my hand up to touch her.

Leda smiled. She bent down and kissed me on the nose. "Horses sweat, men perspire, women glow . . . that's what our gym teacher told us."

It's true.

The next evening, while I was unloading the dishwasher, Dad came into the kitchen. Mom wasn't home from work yet. "So, we met the Boroffs," he said.

"How'd it go?" I asked.

"She's an interesting woman," Dad said. "Very European, somehow, charming in a kind of old world way. But, God, he seemed awfully overbearing!"

"In what way?" I said nervously.

"Well, I said you were thinking of Yale, that I'd gone there and I understood they had a good drama school since Leda's thinking of being an actress. He launched into this real tirade about how Ivy League colleges were all phony, stuffy places and the only way to learn acting was to act and he'd never graduated college and yet he knew more about literature than ten professors of English at Harvard or Yale put together."

I frowned. "I didn't know he'd be like that, Dad . . . I mean, I've met him but—"

"I think it's all oedipal, frankly," Dad said. "He's losing the light of his life and he's freaking out."

"Leda?"

"Sure. . . . Look, I don't blame him. She's an adorable girl. *I* wouldn't want to lose her either."

Neither would I, I thought. "What'd her mother say?"

"She was a lot better. He had about four Scotches and she

kept patting his arm and saying she thought he was exaggerating, that no matter what profession you entered, it was important to have a well-rounded education. She said she thought you were a wonderful young man and had been a good influence on Leda, that she used to spend a lot of time going to parties and dances and now she stayed home and—"

I turned red. I was afraid he was going to say, "and fucked." But he finished, "and studied." God, do I hope Leda isn't pregnant! I don't even want to imagine the scene between Leda's father and mine if he thought she was. I better get out of the country quick if she is. And she used to say she told him everything because he was so understanding!

Dad put his hand on my shoulder. "Joel, fathers of daughters are just . . . It's a whole other ball game. Nan's father never asked me, in fifteen *years,* a single question about myself. Not *one!* I don't think he even knew what profession I was in! I was just some guy who hung around the house, occasionally siring a child and taking her to concerts."

"Would *you* have been like that with a daughter?" I asked, looking up at him.

He smiled. "Maybe. . . . Who knows? I'd like to think not, but you can't tell."

That evening Leda called. "Listen, I want to apologize for Daddy," she said.

"That's okay," I said.

"Mom said he was just awful!" she said. "He can get like that. Like, sometimes he has too much to drink and he starts thinking I'm ten years old or something. . . . He's not *really* like that. He's really a darling, but Mom was afraid your parents might've been offended or something."

"No," I said cautiously, adding, "they liked your mother a lot."

163

"Didn't they think she was horribly old-fashioned?"

"No . . . My father said she was, I forget, very European."

"That's what I mean! . . . Well, she thought your parents were great. She thinks your father is urbane and witty. She said he reminded her of David Niven. . . . And that your mother seems very smart and put together."

David Niven! I wonder if I should tell Dad that. *I* certainly never noticed any special resemblance.

❧ 17 ❧

You're going to find this hard to believe, maybe impossible, but Berger actually went to bed with the lady doctor. I know I should stop calling her the lady doctor, but that's how I think of her. Even when I think of their being in bed, I imagine her with a stethoscope around her neck.

"Look, you don't have to believe me," Berger said after he told me.

"No, I just . . ."

I knew he'd been seeing her pretty often, but I thought she just regarded him as a friend, someone to talk to who wouldn't have any interest in her in terms of sex. "How did it happen?" I said. "I mean, I thought you just talked."

"We did . . . and this is what's weird. Remember when we studied the Middle Ages, there was that thing about knights having these crushes on women they regarded as unattainable?''

"Courtly love?" I remembered. It had never sounded that convincing to me.

"Well, the thing is, I think one reason I turned off so many girls was I was so much on the make. I really acted obnoxious. All I thought of when I was with them was how to get them into bed. They thought I was awful. I was! I used to go home understanding perfectly how they felt. If any of them had done it with me, I'd have thought they were total jerks!''

I found this really interesting. I'd always thought of Berger as someone who was extremely successful with girls. I knew he'd never had sex with anyone but Marilyn Globerman, but I thought that was more because he hadn't met anyone that terrific or maybe he'd done everything but with dozens. "So, with her you acted different?''

"Yeah! I was so scared she'd confuse me with those slobs at the hospital, and also, well, it *was* great having her to talk to. I mean, she seemed really interested in everything I said. And since sex was ruled out—I felt guilty even *thinking* about it when I was with her!—that meant we talked about just about everything. Not just me! She talked a lot too.''

"So, how did you get from talking to sex?''

Berger smiled. "Well, we had dinner one night; she cooked something and we smoked a few joints. I guess I was so relaxed, I forgot and said something about not wanting to go to college next year. I tried to cover it up, but she said, 'I know you're in high school.' Listen to this! She'd known it all along! She knew from that night she took me to the hospital because they needed ID and she searched my pockets and found all this stuff from school.''

"And she didn't mind?''

"Well, I guess she didn't think it would lead anywhere necessarily. . . . And, this is interesting, her father is four

166

years younger than her mother and she says they're the happiest couple she ever knew!" Berger's face was shining. "They sound terrific. I might fly out to Oregon with her this summer and meet them."

I put up my hand. "Wait. . . . You mean, this is really serious?"

Berger looked at me like I was crazy. "No, I'm just horsing around. . . . What's *wrong* with you? It's the most serious thing that ever happened to me! Don't you listen?"

"I do, but—"

"I'm going to *marry* her!" Berger said. "I don't care if I have to wait till she's seventy-five and I'm sixty-eight. I'll wait till I'm eighty-eight! You want to know something? You know, I consider myself a realist, right? Even sort of cynical, maybe, certainly not like you, kind of dreamy and vague and—"

"Hey," I protested, but he raised his hand.

"Okay, scratch the dreamy and vague. But don't you basically think of me as fairly down-to-earth?"

I nodded. This was not accounting for Berger's manic streak, but I decided this wasn't the time to mention that.

"Well, Ingrid . . . There's no other girl I want and there never will be. That's it. The bottom line. I mean, I really believe that we were destined to meet, I believe all that total horseshit that I used to laugh at. . . . And it's all due to you!"

"Me?"

"Yeah, because what if you hadn't wanted me to come along to that Simon and Garfunkel concert? We'd have never met!"

I laughed. "I thought you said it was destined. So you'd have met anyway. . . . Maybe you should be grateful to the beer bottle. What if you hadn't tripped on it?"

"Don't joke. . . . I'm never drinking anything but beer for the rest of my life."

167

I sat thinking about it all, slightly bewildered. "So, wait, what happened after she told you she'd known all along you were in high school?"

Berger grinned. "You want the dirty parts, huh?"

"Sure."

"Well, I got all confused and embarrassed and said I'd only lied because I was scared she wouldn't want to see me if she knew my real age. She said she thought people were whatever age they thought of themselves as, that her grandmother was ninety-four and the youngest person, in spirit, of anyone she knew. God, I love her family! Don't they sound great? A ninety-four-year-old grandmother! Her father's a tool and die worker, whatever that is. They're real, like, *people*. They eat in the kitchen, they grow their own vegetables—"

"They're Jewish, right?"

"Right, for generations back."

"So, your parents won't have a fit?" Berger's parents are much more religiously Jewish than mine. They belong to a temple and go every holiday and have Passover.

"Fuck my parents! . . . I don't *care!* I don't care if no one in my family ever speaks to me again. Hopie's good. She'll love Ingrid, I know it. Everyone'll love her. You can't help it. She's . . . she's just—"

"So, how did you get her into bed?"

"God, you have really changed! You've got a dirty mind, you know that? I'm giving you all this wonderful background material and—"

"You don't have to tell me," I said. "I just meant—"

"I know. . . . It's embarrassing, that's all. Well, she just said, after saying all that stuff about age, that she thought I was a very mature, sensitive, wonderful person and that she sometimes had the feeling that maybe my feelings for her weren't just platonic and she thought it would be best if we talked about it. So I said they weren't. I mean, I didn't say I'd been thinking about nothing else since I met her. I was reasonably cool—for me."

"What'd she say?"

"She just looked at me and smiled. She has such a great smile! God! And she said, 'My feelings aren't totally platonic either.' And then we kind of kissed each other and about three seconds later we were in bed! I was so nervous! It wasn't even . . . I didn't even in some ways enjoy it. I mean, I did, but I just had this strange feeling like it wasn't really happening, or even that it was some kind of a joke or that she'd disappear."

I remember feeling something like that with Leda. "I know what you mean," I said. I suddenly realized Berger hadn't been smoking while we were talking. It was practically the first conversation we'd had in the last three years where he hadn't smoked. "Aren't you smoking anymore?" I asked him.

"Well, you won't believe this either, but I gave it up. Or I'm trying to, anyway; I break down occasionally. No, it's just Ingrid said she was really concerned about my health, and she'd had a cousin who died of lung cancer at thirty-four and she lay awake at night, worried about me. . . . So, what could I do? I'm a reformed character! I told her I'd go to college, if any place will have me. I won't get mad at Mr. Jazinski. I even went up to Jazinski last week and told him I was really sorry I'd caused him all this grief, that there'd been some family problems that I didn't feel free to discuss and I was sorry I'd taken it out in class. He said all was forgiven, he knew I had great potential and he was really pleased because he'd been afraid I'd end up assassinating a president or something. God, the guy's nuts!"

I laughed. I'd never told Berger about the lecture Mr. Jazinski had given all of us that day he stormed out of class.

I was glad about what had happened to Berger, not just because he's my friend and he seems so happy. But also, it was April fourth and a week before my birthday. At this point in my life, my birthday doesn't have any great significance for me. But this year it means I know whether I'm going to be a father. Or could be. I just haven't wanted to talk about that, even with Berger. It's not that he wouldn't be sympathetic. I guess in some way I'm being like Leda, hoping that if I don't confront it, it'll disappear.

My parents gave me two hundred dollars for my birthday. They said I could do anything I wanted with it, save it, spend it, or whatever. I think I'll buy a new stereo. The one I have is okay, but it's basically kind of cheesy and if you like music, a good system can make a big difference.

My brithday came on a Tuesday so I had school. After school I went over to Berger's. I didn't get back till almost six. My parents were taking me out to dinner at Windows on the World, this fancy restaurant downtown that has a great view of the city. As I came in my mother said, "Oh, Joel, Leda called."

My heart sank. About a second later, she said, "You better hurry, dear. Our reservation is at six thirty. . . . You got a letter too. It's on your desk."

I figured the letter was probably from my Aunt Muriel, who always sends me cards on my birthday and Christmas. I opened it up. It was a Father's Day card. Inside it said: "To the best father ever, much love on this very special day." It was just signed "L." And at the bottom, "P.S. Happy Birthday."

Shit. I just stood there for a long time, holding the card. Then I put it back in the envelope and stuffed it away in the drawer of my desk. My mother called out again, "Joel, please hurry. I mean it!"

I decided to call Leda later, after we got back. I didn't really feel like talking to her, actually. It seemed like such a dumb thing to do, sending a card like that on my birthday. Maybe she thought it was funny. But why couldn't she have waited till after my birthday? Just a day after. I tried not to think about it while we had dinner, but I couldn't. The food was good and the view was terrific, but I couldn't really enjoy it or pay much attention. My parents were talking about how we'd all fly out to L.A. next week for Knox's wedding.

"This time next week I'll be a mother-in-law," my mother said.

"*I'll* be a father-in-law," my father said.

"That doesn't sound so bad," my mother said. "Mother-in-law sounds so—"

"You'll be terrific," my father said.

They both seemed in a basically good mood. I wished I could be too.

"How do *you* feel about Knox getting married?" Mom asked, turning to me.

"Okay," I said.

"I hope they'll be happy," she went on.

"Why shouldn't they be?" Dad asked.

"I don't know. . . . So many people seem *not* to be these days. It's all so iffy."

"Look at us," Dad said. "We've lasted."

"That's what I mean," Mom said. "We have, but who knows why? It's all so mysterious."

Dad raised his glass. He'd ordered champagne because of my birthday. "To the mystery of life," he said.

I was glad when we got home. It was past ten. I lay on my bed. I didn't want to call Leda and I knew that was cowardly. It wasn't that I didn't want to spoil my birthday because it had been spoiled already. I just knew I felt angry at her and I was afraid it would show if we spoke. Anyway, I figured she might be in bed since she goes to bed early school nights. But at around ten forty-five, just as I'd gotten into bed with the lights off, my mother knocked on my door. "Joel, it's Leda. Are you asleep?"

"No, I'll get it." I got out of bed and went into the kitchen, closing the door firmly behind me. "Hi," I said. "We just got back from dinner. I'm sorry I didn't have a chance to call earlier."

"Did you get my note?"

"Yeah."

"I'm sorry it had to be on your birthday," Leda said.

"That's okay."

There was a pause.

"Listen, would you like to eat out Saturday? I thought I might take you out for your birthday."

"My parents already did."

"I know! But this would be my treat. You said you liked Japanese food and there's this really good place my parents told me about down here."

"Sure," I said, trying to sound more enthusiastic than I felt. "That sounds good."

When I got off the phone, I felt lousy. I wasn't sure if Leda had sensed how I felt. Usually she's pretty sensitive about my moods, which can be either a good or a bad thing. The trouble was, I still felt angry and it wasn't just her letting me know on my birthday. It was the whole thing. Okay, I'm not a girl and so obviously I can't totally imagine what it's like to make love, knowing it might lead to pregnancy. But I think if I was, I'd have been a lot more careful than Leda was. She could have told me she left her diaphragm at home that time we were here—I had those condoms. I could have used them. She hates it when I say men are more organized than women and plan ahead better. Maybe they don't always, but it seems to me if men got pregnant, they'd be more careful. You wouldn't even need to *have* abortions. Leda says if men got pregnant, abortion would be a sacrament. She read that in some feminist magazine.

172

❧ 18 ❧

I went to Leda's house on Saturday since she'd said the restaurant was near there. When I got there, she was still getting dressed. Her father was in the living room, reading. He was the last person on earth I wanted to see!

"Hi, Joel," he said.

I read about ten different meanings into that pretty banal greeting. Leda couldn't have told him, I figured. She couldn't have. If she had, he would have leaped at my throat and torn me limb from limb. I'm pretty positive he didn't know anything.

"I enjoyed meeting your parents the other night," he said.

That was surprising. I didn't get that feeling from what my father said. "Yeah, well, they enjoyed it too," I said.

"Your mother knows a great deal about the theater," he

said. "She seems like a very sensitive, educated person. I mean, in the intuitive sense. She understands plays very well."

"They go to the theater a lot," I said.

There was a pause. I guess he wasn't going to say anything about my father.

"Have you made any definite plans about next year?" Mr. Boroff asked.

"Uh . . . you mean college?"

"Right. . . . You said you'd been thinking of Paris."

I winced. "Well, that doesn't look too . . . My parents said maybe I could spend the summer there. But they're pretty concerned about my starting college in the fall."

"Where do you think you'll go?"

"I haven't decided for sure."

"Leda got a scholarship at Yale," he said. "I guess she told you."

She hadn't. "That's where my father went," I said.

"I have nothing against Yale," Mr. Boroff said. "I have nothing against Harvard or Princeton. It's just half the guys you meet who went to those places, they act like they expect the world to be handed to them on a platter. They went to Yale so supposedly that makes them an intellectual. Bullshit! A man is what he makes of himself, not where he went to school. . . . My grandfather never learned to read or write and he's the smartest man I ever met. He came to this country when he was thirteen, an orphan, and in ten years he had the biggest flower business in Boston!"

"I probably won't even get in," I said.

"Go! Get in!" he said, as if it were up to me. "A good education can't hurt you. It just won't do it for you either, you know what I mean?"

"Sure," I said.

Just then Leda came out of her room. She was wearing this strange style that, according to her, is "in" this year:

knickers that are like pants that come down to her knees and sort of puff out, and this very lacy, old-fashioned blouse, gold stockings, and gold slippers. I know for Leda, maybe because she wants to be an actress, clothes are kind of, well, not just a way to keep yourself warm. She looked really pretty, but it was almost like a costume. Her father eyed her approvingly. "Do I have a beautiful daughter or don't I?" he said.

"You look nice," I said to her.

He sighed. "Joel, let me give you a piece of advice. Don't have a beautiful daughter. You'll never have a peaceful night. I don't mean you, you're a nice, sincere young man, but pretty girls attract the most nutty, schmege-gy guys you'd ever want to see. Now, I'm lucky in one respect. Leda has good taste . . . sometimes. She—"

"Daddy, shut up," Leda said, but good-naturedly. She kissed him.

"Would I have told my father to shut up?" Mr. Boroff asked me. "He'd have knocked me to kingdom come." He looked up lovingly at Leda. "I'm putty in her hands."

"Daddy, I mean it!" She got her coat from the closet. "You didn't even wish Joel a happy birthday. It's his birthday."

"All the best," Mr. Boroff said, waving. "Have fun, kids."

"Don't mind him," Leda said when we were outside.

"I don't." I hesitated a second. "You didn't . . . tell him about—"

She looked at me in horror. "Are you crazy? Don't you value your life?"

I swallowed. "Yeah, well . . . you once said he was so understanding. But I'm glad you didn't."

"He'd have a cow! . . . He *hated* your father! Listen, don't take it personally. *I* think he's great. But Daddy said how he kept going on about gourmet food and wine and—"

"He always does that," I said.

"I know! I told Daddy, 'That's just his profession,' but I guess he thought your father was sort of lording it over him. Daddy said, 'I come from peasant stock and I'm proud of it. I'd rather have a brisket of beef than a boeuf anything any day of the week.'" Leda can mimic her father to a T, his voice, his gestures, everything.

At this point we were at the restaurant. It was a dark, quiet place. We looked at the menus a long time. Leda told me what she thought was good. They were all slightly strange things made with raw fish and seaweed. We ordered wine with it. When it came, Leda raised her glass.

"To your scholarship at Yale," I said.

She blushed. "I was going to tell you about that, but—"

"That's okay."

"Did you hear yet?"

"I got on the waiting list. . . . And I got into Hampshire and Wesleyan."

"Those are good places," Leda said quickly, but I knew she'd have said that no matter what places they were.

"I'll probably go to Wesleyan. . . . Mom and Dad think Hampshire isn't structured enough."

"Yeah, I've heard that." She smiled. "Well, happy birthday, anyway!"

"Thanks."

We sipped our wine. It was awkward, like we were on a first date or even a blind date. I took a deep breath. "I'm sorry about—"

"Oh, listen, don't worry," Leda said quickly, interrupting me. "It's okay. It's all fixed up. It's not a big deal, Joel, really. Danny's sister had one once. They just kind of vacuum you out. They give you this local anesthetic so you don't even feel it. Maybe just for one second, she said. . . . And then I'll go on the Pill, which I should've

176

done at the beginning." She was talking very fast and cheerfully, but I could tell that wasn't how she felt.

"I still feel bad," I said.

"Don't. . . . Really, it's *my* fault. I'm just careless."

"I'd like to be with you when you have it."

Leda looked touched. "Yeah, I'd . . . I'd like you to."

"When is it? I mean, did you make an appointment yet?"

"A week from Wednesday at four."

"Oh, shit."

"What?"

"I'll be in L.A. . . . My brother's getting married."

Leda frowned. "I thought he was getting married in June."

"No, he was going to, but they switched it to April. . . . You were there, remember? It's because her parents got married in April or something."

"I thought it was the other way around. They were going to do it in April, but her parents got married in June."

"No, it's the way I said."

"Are you sure?"

"Of course I'm sure."

"I remembered it the other way around."

"Well, you remembered it wrong."

Leda just stared at me. "So, what will we do?"

"Well, I've got to go to the wedding, Lee. . . . You can understand that, can't you?"

"You mean, you'd rather go to the wedding than be with me?" Her voice quavered.

"No! It's just my parents would have a fit. It's my only brother. It's not that I *want* to go, it's that—"

"Can't you get out of it? Make some excuse?"

"What excuse?" I felt really angry. I couldn't figure out why she was acting this way. "The truth?"

Leda looked down, like she was going to cry. "Well, I guess I'll just go by myself," she said.

"Can't you rearrange it?" I said, trying not to sound exasperated. "I'll be back Wednesday night. Just make it for Friday."

"I don't know if you can," she said with a very worried expression.

"Of course you can! What if you'd been sick?"

"But the thing is, I've waited so long already!" Leda said. "Every day I wait, it's more of a real baby. I mean, before it was just a little clump of cells or whatever and now it probably has fingernails and toes and . . ."

"You should've done it earlier." I guess I shouldn't have said that, but it's true.

Leda started to cry. "I know!" she said. "Stop being mad at me! I feel awful enough already."

Seeing her cry made me feel terrible. I got up and sat down next to her. Even though there were other people eating right near us, I put my arms around her. I kissed her. "Lee, don't cry . . . I'll—we'll figure something out."

"You have to go to the wedding."

"Maybe I can think of something."

"No . . . listen, I can change it. It's only two extra days." Even while she was talking, tears kept dripping down her cheeks.

God, I felt rotten! It's true part of it *was* Leda's fault, her carelessness and her waiting that extra month, but still part of it was due to me. You can't get around that.

"Do you think I should have the baby?" Leda asked in a very low voice, looking down at her lap.

"No."

"There aren't that many Jewish babies," she said, sniffing, trying to smile. "There'd be nine million people who'd want it. I could probably sell it for a year's tuition at Yale."

"I thought you had a scholarship." I tried to joke.

"For four years' tuition!" She looked over at me, more

her regular self. "No, listen, I don't really want to. It just seems so grisly to me, having a baby and then having to give it away like that. You'd spend all your life worrying about the people that adopted it. I mean, what if they were mean people? Or just dumb people? People who never went to the theater or who were Moral Majority types who believed in hitting their kids? And what if your kid came to you when it was twenty and it had turned into this awful person just because it'd been raised that way? . . . Or what if it was mad at you for having given it up for adoption?"

Leda can get slightly carried away at times. I was holding her hand. I squeezed it. "It's going to be okay," I said, trying to act the way I imagined my brother would under similar circumstances.

At that point the waiter arrived with our food. I moved back to my seat. It all tasted slightly odd to me. I guess raw fish isn't my thing. Or maybe our conversation had slightly taken my appetite away.

"I thought you liked Japanese food," Leda said, noticing me shoving some things to one side of my plate.

What I'd been thinking of when I'd said that was this Japanese steak house I'd gone to a few times with my father where they had this really tender steak. He said the cows aren't allowed to move, even, and they're massaged every day and drink beer, which supposedly makes their meat especially tender. That was before I was a vegetarian. "It's good," I said.

Leda seemed really hungry. She took some of the stuff I didn't eat. "It's lucky I don't have a weight problem," she said.

After dinner we went back to her house. Leda gave me the present she'd made for me. She'd made it in school. It was a two-inch gold guitar, really beautiful, everything on it, the strings, the hollow in the center. I guess I can use it as a paperweight. "Thanks," I said. I hadn't expected she would actually make something for me.

After that we lay down on her bed, our arms around each other. Leda said, "Joel, this might sound strange, but is it okay if we don't do it till after I have the abortion? I just feel—"

"Sure." Actually, I felt the same way. Also, it's only thirteen days, a week of which I'll be away, so it doesn't seem like such a sacrifice.

"I guess the only thing is you wonder—what if he or she had grown up to be someone terrific, some great poet or scientist or something?" Leda said. "Or just, like, a really nice person."

"I think it's better not to think about it," I said.

"Yeah, I guess."

We lay there together and after a while Leda fell asleep. Maybe she was worn out from all the emotion of the evening. I felt sleepy myself, but I didn't actually fall asleep. I just lay there, with my arms around her. Leda looks young when she's sleeping, more like Hopie. She has this way of pressing her hand up against her mouth and she breathes in that heavy, even way little kids do. It was hard for me to keep feeling mad at her.

I'm not much looking forward to L.A.

❧ 19 ❧

Once I got to L.A. it was different. In fact, even when we were in the airport, getting ready to board the plane, I was excited and glad to be going away. I felt bad about this, but really I was glad to be getting away from Leda. I just don't feel like spending any more time talking about this baby! About whether it might've been Einstein or might've been a mongoloid. What's the point? Maybe that's insensitive. Maybe if it were a baby growing inside me, I'd feel differently. I don't know. But I think I'm just a more practical person than Leda. If I don't see the point in doing something, I don't do it. Whereas she does.

Anyhow, I told her I'd call her while I was there, but when you're in a totally different place, with different people, everything at home seems pretty far away.

One thing always strikes me when we visit my brother

that normally I don't think about that much. My brother has really made it financially. You should see this house he lives in. It's in a canyon, has a huge garden and a view for hundreds of miles. The living room is twice as big as my parents' living room! There are terraces. There's a bathroom with a rosewood tub; you can take a bath looking out at the mountains. Okay, so money isn't everything. My father isn't earning anything like what Knox is earning and neither is my mother and they always say you shouldn't enter a profession because of how much money you're going to earn. But still, I always get the feeling they're pretty impressed when they visit him. And it makes me wonder because I have the feeling I'm not going to be like that. I'll probably earn half what my father does! I just don't care about money that much. I don't want to live like a bum, but I know I'll never ever be able to afford a house like this one. And I wish I didn't care that I'm afraid my parents will compare us and say why isn't Joel like Knox?

We arrived Sunday night. Monday there was a rehearsal for the wedding and we met Angelica's family. I don't know why, but her mother reminded me of this woman on a spaghetti commercial on TV. She had dark blond hair and she was pretty, a little overweight, but she had this hearty, sincere way of talking. When she met me, she said, "Look at him! Handsomer than his brother! Angie, go get the girls. They'll go wild."

Angelica dragged out her two sisters who were twelve and fourteen. They were both a little chubby with that same friendly smile. One of them had braces. "We went to New York once and we got mugged," the older one said accusingly, as though it was my fault.

"It was noisy," the other one said.

That kind of ended the conversation. Angelica's father was this very tall, bald man with a deep voice who shook your hand till you thought it was going to drop off. "That's some brother you have," he said to me. "He's got a real head for business. I guess it runs in the family, huh?"

Actually, I don't think it does, but I just said, "Yeah, I guess so."

"I never thought I'd see the day when I'd be glad to see Angie married," he said. "None of them were ever good enough for her. That's how I looked at it. But your brother— I took one look at him and thought, 'That's the guy for Angie.' I knew it right off the bat. I told her the first evening she brought him home. I said, 'Angie, that's the one. Grab him before he gets away.'"

I think I'm going to elope if I ever get married. I don't think I could take the whole thing with parents and in-laws and sisters and brothers.

The rehearsal went okay. To tell the truth, I wasn't listening that much because there wasn't much I had to do. Knox's best friend, Sterling Colp, was best man and one of Angie's friends was her best whatever they call it. Sterling was Knox's roommate in college. He's a dentist too. He's short and funny-looking, sort of like a leprechaun. Angie's best friend was a real knockout. I mean, almost unreal. The best figure I've ever seen and a really pretty face with black curly hair and slightly tilted black eyes, like she might have been part Oriental. I hoped Knox wouldn't run off with her. He was kind of eyeing her at times, but hopefully no one but me noticed. What a jerk! He's getting married tomorrow and he's still eyeing other women.

When we got back from the rehearsal, I got a great idea. I decided to call Lassie Bligen. She's that girl who I started to like and who started to like me in camp the summer before this past one. It's true that was almost two years ago, but I thought she'd still remember me. Also, for some reason I remember her address, maybe because it was a funny name. She lives on Cottontail Lane. She said it sounded like something out of a Disney movie; she's right. I found her number in the L.A. phone book and went in to call her.

She answered the phone. I could recognize her voice. "Hello?"

"Uh, Lassie? . . . This is Joel Davis. I don't know if you remember me, but—"

"Oh, Joel. . . . Gee, how great! Where *are* you? You sound so close!"

She sounded so enthusiastic that I felt really good. I told her about my brother's wedding and how I'd be around for three days and I wondered if I could see her.

"Sure, I'd love to. . . . Could you come over tonight? Do you have some way of getting here?"

I told her where my brother's house was and she said that wasn't too far from where she lived. I asked my parents and they said they could drop me off before they went out for dinner with some people they know. "So, I'll see you around eight," I said.

"Terrific! . . . I'm so excited! I can hardly wait."

The thing about Lassie that was always true was that she was a very enthusiastic, friendly person who seemed to get a kick out of a lot of things. When I used to see her in the Pub Shop, writing her poetry, she'd be so absorbed, she wouldn't even notice I was there. Once, I tapped her lightly on the shoulder and she jumped sky high. But she never minded being interrupted. Anyway, I felt really good that she was so pleased to hear from me. Two years is a kind of long time and she might've practically forgotten who I was.

She looked pretty much the same. I've grown about four inches since then so whereas before we were almost the same height, now I'm quite a bit taller. She'd cut her hair, but it was still thick and shaggy with bangs that hung down almost into her eyes. She's not pretty the way Leda is, not sexy exactly, but she has a nice face. She hugged me. "You look so different," she said. "I practically wouldn't have recognized you."

"Really?"

"Do I, to you? I cut my hair, only I decided to let it grow again."

"It looks nice," I said. Actually, I liked it better long. She brought me into her parents' den. It had a big fireplace. I wondered why people would need a fireplace in L.A. It never seems that cold. Lassie curled up on the sofa, her knees tucked under her. "So, are you still doing a lot with music?" she asked.

"Pretty much." Actually that summer I was a lot better than I am now. I used to practice every day for at least two hours. I even gave a concert at camp where I'd written three of the songs myself.

"Those songs you wrote were so pretty!" Lassie said. "You said you were going to be a songwriter."

"Maybe I still will." I told her about how I'd thought of taking the year off to go to Paris, but was only going for summer vacation instead.

"Hey, neat!" she said, almost bouncing up and down with excitement. "I'll be in Paris too. I'm going for two months on the Experiment in International Living. Did you ever hear of it?"

I shook my head.

"It's this thing where you live with a French family for a month and then bicycle around some other part of France. My family is in Normandy and we're bicycling around the Mediterranean, but I think we have a week in Paris. We could meet! Would you like to?"

"Sure."

"How's your French? Is it really good?"

"Fair . . . but my father says once you get there and start speaking, you get better fast."

"I've been trying to read all these novels in French just

for practice. This friend of my mother sent me a novel for teen-agers that I'd read in English! It was so different in French! Like, in English this guy said, 'I'm a feminist,' and in French they translated it as 'I love women!' " She laughed. "The best one was in English they said, 'They were up half the night making love,' and in French it said, 'They consecrated half the night to their amorous games.' " She laughed again. She has a great laugh. It just kind of booms out.

I laughed too. Her talking about sex made me start to think about it, though. Maybe it had the same effect on her because suddenly there was an awkward pause. "Do you have a girl friend?" she asked.

I swallowed. "Yeah, kind of," I said. I really hated myself for adding "kind of." It was a reflex action. Kind of! Here I'd been seeing someone steadily all year and gotten her pregnant. Some "kind of"!

"Who is she?" Lassie was always extremely interested in people.

"She's . . . she lives in New York, but she goes to a different school from me."

"Is it, like, serious?"

I nodded. "How about you?" I asked.

She looked away a minute. "Well, I was going with someone, but we've kind of broken up. I mean, we still see each other, but . . . I guess partly it's that we'll be at different schools next year. I'm going to Wellesley and he's going to Stanford so it would be a little tricky, but it's also—" She looked up at me. "Well, it's . . . are you, um, sleeping with your girl friend? I don't mean to be overly personal, but—"

"Yeah, we are," I said, feeling uncomfortable.

"Well, the thing is, maybe it's different with you, I guess it's different with everyone, but with us . . . Maybe we weren't ready or something. I don't know! I feel really confused about it. It was like we were close in lots of ways, but maybe that put too much pressure on the whole thing. He started to feel that I was sort of closing in on him. . . . And I was, sort of! I'm just a horribly jealous person. It's a real character defect. We'd go to parties and he'd flirt with other girls, not even meaning anything, and I'd feel so bad."

"I know what you mean," I said.

"It's just so confusing," Lassie said. "I think we really loved each other, but—"

"Yeah." Here's what was awful. I started really feeling attracted to her. Partly it was having the feeling she felt that way about me. I don't know how you can tell, but you can. And also, the same things I had liked about her in camp two years ago I still liked, the way she just told you whatever she was feeling in that very direct, straightforward way.

There was a long pause. I felt divided in two. Part of me wanted to lean over and kiss her. She was maybe six inches away and her eyes were fixed on me, like she was waiting and hoping I would. But then I thought of Leda and I just couldn't. "Do you still write poetry?" I said, just to say something.

"Yeah, I even had something published," she said. She jumped up. "It's going to be in this little magazine. You don't get paid or anything, but still I felt really great about it."

"Could I see it?"

"Sure. . . . Come up to my room. I'll show you the ones I think are really good." As we went upstairs, she turned around and asked, "Do you still write, Joel? You used to be so good! You were so talented at everything."

"Not so much anymore."

She had a big room with a bunk bed, a gigantic desk with a typewriter on it, and a green bean-bag chair in one corner.

"I love my desk," she said. "I hope there's room for it in my room at college."

I read about twenty of her poems. She's really good. I don't mean just good like a kid our age can be good, but good like I can imagine she might even publish a book someday. Some of them were hard to understand, but she explained them to me. Most of the ones we studied in school were hard too. "I guess poetry has to be hard to understand," I said.

"It shouldn't be," Lassie said. "It should be complicated, but not hard."

We were sitting together side by side on the floor. Just a second after she said that we turned and kissed. It was like it happened before I even stopped to think or tried to stop. Afterward we looked at each other. "Help," Lassie said.

"My girl friend's pregnant," I blurted out, God knows why. "I shouldn't even be here. I feel like a shit."

"The trouble with the world," she said, frowning, "is there are so many people you can like or love even."

"I know." I thought about Knox and Angelica and whether they would stay married a long time, like my parents.

"What I mean is," Lassie said, "we like each other. We did before and we still do. That doesn't make us terrible people."

I sighed. "I don't know."

"Is your girl friend nice?"

"Yeah."

It was like the whole room was vibrating. I think one major problem with having sex with one girl is it's hard not to realize that you can do it with another one. You know it's not impossible, that they might even want to too. I felt like we were about one second away from that. I jumped up. "Let's go for a walk," I said.

The good thing about Lassie is she seems to understand

things. She just smiled at me and said she'd like to. We took a long walk around her neighborhood. Once we were outside, out of range of a bed, it was a lot easier. Not that it's not possible to do it out of doors, but it was like the air was cleared.

"I've thought of you a lot," Lassie said. "I even wanted to write you, but I wasn't sure you wanted me to."

"Sure, I'd have liked it."

"Do you want to now? We could. I love writing letters!"

I don't love it so much, but I wanted to stay in touch with her. "We'll meet in Paris," I said. That sounded romantic. I thought of that line she'd quoted, "They consecrated half the night to their amorous games." I wonder what that means. It sounds more complicated and interesting than just screwing. Maybe it's a colloquial expression.

The wedding was the next day. The ceremony part took place in a church. After that we went back to Angelica's parents' house. A lot of people came over. First there was a long line of people who wanted to shake hands with Angelica and Knox and everyone in her family and everyone in our family. I must have shaken hands with about a hundred people! A lot of the people got my parents' professions mixed up. They thought Mom was a gourmet food critic and Dad ran an art gallery. The first few times Dad corrected them, but after a while he just said, yes, running an art gallery is difficult, and Mom said, yes, she did like cooking gourmet things at home, even though she wrote about it. The weirdest thing was this little old guy, some uncle or something, who thought I was Knox. Knox had disappeared for a few minutes and this guy came over to me and said, "You take good care of her, young man, you hear me?"

I just nodded.

"I've known Angelica since she was a baby. I'm her godfather, and I want to tell you there isn't a sweeter, nicer,

189

kinder, brighter girl in the whole world. You treat her right!"

"Sure," I said. I wonder what people mean when they say that. Don't beat her? Don't be mean? You'd think everyone would at least start out in marriage intending to act right.

After the hand-shaking part we had to pose for a lot of photos. The only good part about that was I got to stand right near Angelica's friend, the Oriental girl named Kim. She was even prettier close up than she'd seemed the other day. In one photo they told me to put my arm around her! She had a really tiny waist and incredible breasts. She was wearing one of those filmy dresses where you can imagine pretty well what's underneath. When they started playing dance music, I asked her if she wanted to dance. She wasn't taller than me. She wasn't much taller than Leda, in fact. It was a little hard talking to her, though. She kept looking around the room at other people and if I said anything, she'd say, "Yes?" almost like she hadn't understood what I said.

"You can marry one of Angelica's sisters," she said to me. They were hovering around, looking like they wanted someone to ask them to dance.

"I have a girl friend," I said quickly.

"Why only one?"

I turned red.

"I have three boyfriends," she said cheerfully. "One is for this and one is for that and one is for whatever else I like to do. It's easier that way." She smiled at me. She had perfect little teeth, like pearls.

To me it didn't sound easier, it sounded a lot more complicated.

Just to be a good guy and partly because my mother forced me, I danced with Angelica's sisters who, one, can't dance and, two, are spoiled little slobs, if you ask *my* opinion. One of them said, "You're not as handsome as your brother." The other one said, "Are *you* rich too?"

Knox and Angelica looked pretty happy. I have to say that. They kept kissing each other, even after the ceremony was over, and holding hands. They looked the way you imagine people in love ought to look. At the end of the party they took off. They were flying to Hawaii for two weeks. Knox had left my parents the key to his house so we could stay as long as we wanted.

The night of the wedding we got back to the house around midnight. My mother looked exhausted. "Joel, do me a favor and elope," she said.

"Don't worry," I said.

"How many relatives does that girl have?" my father said.

"Well, her mother is one of seven, her father is one of nine, and I gather the infant mortality rate was horribly low."

"Jesus!" my father said. "I want to sleep for two days straight."

"Did you have fun, Joel?" my mother asked.

"Pretty much," I said.

"It was nice of you to dance with her sisters."

"Yeah," I admitted. "It was."

My father laughed.

The next day we just hung around and recovered. I decided I better call Leda. The thought of her had been hovering at the back of my mind. She answered the phone right away.

"Oh, hi," she said, but she sounded slightly cool. "How are you?"

"Okay. . . . How're you?"

"Good . . . I've been sleeping a lot. I guess it's . . . oh, and Danny and I saw *Cloud Nine*. It was great. . . . So, how was the wedding?"

191

"It was good. . . . They're in Hawaii now."

There was a pause.

"Meet any pretty girls?" Leda asked.

"No, not especially."

"I thought you might've looked up that girl, the one you liked in camp two years ago."

God, women have fantastic memories! I'd just mentioned Lassie once! "I've been kind of busy," I stammered.

Leda laughed. "You're a terrible liar, Joel. . . . That's one of the nice things about you."

"I miss you," I said. That hadn't been exactly true, but hearing her voice, I did.

"I miss you too." Her voice sounded warm and a little trembly.

"We're flying back tomorrow."

"I know."

"I'll call you as soon as I get back. . . . Did you, uh, change the appointment?"

"It's Friday at four. . . . Is that okay for you?"

"Sure."

I hung up, feeling lousy. I wished I hadn't even gone to see Lassie. Why am I even thinking about other girls when I've got Leda? It seemed like a worse thing to do when she was pregnant. I know nothing happened, but in my thoughts they did. When I went home that night after seeing Lassie and jerked off, I thought of her the whole time, not Leda. Okay, so no one has control over their thoughts, but still, if I hadn't seen her, I wouldn't have even had those thoughts. Shit.

Just before we left, about an hour before, Lassie called. I'd given her my brother's phone number. "I wrote you a letter already," she said. "Maybe it'll be there when you get home."

"What did you say?" I didn't think she'd have that much

to say since it's only been a day or so since we'd seen each other.

"Oh, nothing much. It was just, like, a continuation of the conversation we had. I wrote a poem about it."

I've never written much to anyone. I hope I won't feel too self-conscious writing to Lassie, her being a writer and all.

❧ 20 ❧

Maybe everything in life is like that story about "The good part is . . . and the bad part is . . ." The good part is that by Friday evening Leda won't be pregnant anymore. The bad part is that the abortion costs two hundred dollars and I agreed to pay half so there goes my new stereo. I feel like a louse even minding sacrificing the hundred dollars. It's true, as Leda says, no matter how I feel about it, I don't actually have to go through an operation. I'm glad of that. I hate even having teeth pulled and minor stuff like that.

When I got back to New York, even though the letter from Lassie was there, waiting for me, the whole time in L.A. seemed extremely remote, like it had happened a long time ago. I told Berger on the phone about Leda's being pregnant and my going with her to have the abortion. It seemed easier telling him on the phone.

"Is it a good place?" he asked.

"I guess . . . I think she checked it out."

"I could ask Ingrid, if you want."

Berger thinks Ingrid knows everything there is to know about everything! I didn't feel like having a whole lot of other people know about it. I told him that. "Okay," he said. "No sweat. . . . How's she taking it?"

"Pretty well, I guess." I'm not really sure how Leda's taking it. She seemed more upset at the beginning, when she knew for sure she was pregnant. But since she decided to have the abortion, she's been more quiet and a little removed.

We went to the clinic by subway. It was way uptown, around 168th Street. It was connected to a hospital. The waiting room wasn't too big, but there were about twenty people in it. We hung up our jackets and sat down to wait. Leda spoke to a woman at the front desk who had her fill out a form. While she was doing that, I looked around the room. Most of the people there looked around our age, which surprised me. I'd thought there'd be more older women with their husbands. There was just one woman who looked over thirty and she had a little kid with her. Quite a few girls were by themselves. They didn't look like Leda. What I mean by that is most of them looked sort of forlorn, not that pretty, not that well off financially. I thought of that expression "knocked up." These girls looked like they'd been "knocked up," like someone had done something to them in a dark alley that they hadn't much enjoyed.

"They give you a local anesthetic," Leda said, after she was done with the form. "I guess it's like Novocain, or something. . . . Did you ever have a tooth pulled?"

"Yeah, I hated it."

"Really? . . . I loved it. They gave me some kind of gas and it was the most terrific feeling, like I was flying. I wish they'd give you that kind of stuff here." She looked around the room. Then she took a piece of paper and wrote on it, "God, look at them!" I wrote back, "I know." I think we were both feeling a variation on the same thing, that we didn't want to think of ourselves like the other people in this room. Like the fact that we were bright and went to good schools and were going to good colleges should have made us smart enough for this not to have happened.

"I saw this movie while you were in California," Leda said in a soft voice, almost a whisper, "about this girl who was adopted and then, when she was, like, my age, she went to look for her real parents. And she was so mad at her mother for giving her up for adoption! So what would be the point? Just to have someone mad at you? She wasn't even happy that the woman had had her!"

"Well, I guess people react different ways," I said.

"If it was you, what would *you* have done?" Leda asked.

That's pretty hard to imagine, but I said, "The same thing you're doing."

"You wouldn't feel guilty or anything?"

"No, not especially."

Leda frowned. "I don't know if I do or not! I think I more feel mad at myself for fucking up." She giggled. "Pardon the expression. . . . And what's weird is it seems the second people get married and *want* to have babies, they can't. They try and try and they just can't!"

"Yeah," I said. "I've heard about that."

"I'm just such a coward about pain," she said. "I wish they'd, like, put you out entirely, like when you have open-heart surgery."

"It won't hurt," I said, trying to sound calm and reassuring.

"I know. . . . Still." Then we just sat there for about twenty more minutes, holding hands, till the woman at the

196

front desk called Leda. Her hands were icy cold. She smiled at me nervously and went off.

I sat back and looked around the room again. I'd brought a book with me, but I didn't much feel like reading. I noticed a boy sitting next to me, about my age, playing chess on one of those small sets you can bring on trips. He noticed me studying the board and said, "Do you play?"

"A little." I used to play a lot with Berger a few years ago, but then he stopped being interested and gradually I did too. This guy was Oriental and I had the feeling he'd be really good. That's not a logical deduction. It's just the guy who's the president of the chess club at school was Oriental and he was incredibly good. I know that doesn't mean all Oriental guys are.

"Want to play? You can take either side."

I studied the board. Both sides were about even which I guess tends to happen if you play yourself. I chose white. He beat me, but he wasn't as good as I'd been afraid he'd be. He might still have beaten me, even when I was at my best a few years ago, but he wasn't a genius.

"Was that your girl friend?" he said, nodding in the direction Leda had disappeared. He'd told me his name was Paul.

"Yeah. . . . Who're you waiting for?"

"My sister."

That was unusual, bringing your sister. I tried to imagine Berger with Hopie, but couldn't. "Couldn't her boyfriend come?" I said.

He made a face. "He doesn't know. He lives in England. I wanted her to write him, but she said no. I guess it was pride or something."

"Yeah," I said. I can imagine that.

"She wanted to have the baby, but I talked her out of it. She's only sixteen! . . . She loves babies." He looked at me. "You going to get married or anything?" I must have looked horrified because he laughed and said, "I guess not."

"We're both going to college," I said slowly. It's funny. I've heard of this, how it's easier talking to someone you've never met and know you'll never see again, but I never had that experience until now.

He looked at me for a minute. "I don't have a girl friend," he said. "I never had one. . . . Where are you going to college?"

"Wesleyan."

"Kiki and I have another year. We're twins."

"Where do you go to school now?"

"Hunter."

I guess they must both be pretty smart. It's hard to get in there. He kept staring at me as though there was something he wanted to say. "Listen," he said suddenly. "Um, this is going to sound strange. . . . But how come you . . . I mean, why did your girl friend get pregnant?"

For a minute I wasn't sure what he meant. He seemed a little old not to know the facts of life. "What do you mean?"

"What I mean is . . . do you love her?"

"Yeah."

He looked relieved. "It seems like a lot of guys just . . . they pretend it's love, and sometimes girls are kind of naive, do you know what I mean? My sister's really smart, but this guy she . . . he was awful! He didn't love her. He said he was going to marry her. I don't know why girls fall for that. It's good he went back to England. I would've killed him if I'd seen him again."

"I guess it's different with everyone," I said. But even though I had no reason to, I started feeling guilty. The fact is, I do love Leda and I certainly never said anything to her that I didn't mean, never promised anything I wasn't going to do, but still it's hard to have a clear conscience when it comes to things with girls. You don't even know for sure what your motives really are. Like, I think we really love each other, but maybe that's something you say at a certain point because just saying you want to fuck sounds crude. I don't mean by that that all we wanted from each other was sex, but I didn't feel a hundred percent clear about it.

"How come you don't have a girl friend?" I said.

He smiled. "I don't know. . . . I have a friend who's a girl, but . . ."

"That's different."

"I want to be a doctor. It's a lot of work. Maybe it's better not to get involved with anyone."

That sounded kind of like an excuse to me. I thought of Berger and Ingrid. "I never had one before either," I said. "A girl friend, I mean. It just kind of happened."

"Kiki was too young," he said. "I'm not saying that just because I'm her brother. She should have waited."

"Well . . ." What can you say to that? Especially when I'd never met her *or* the guy she did it with. At that moment the door opened and an Oriental girl came out and walked over to us. Paul jumped up and took her arm. "How was it?" he said anxiously. "Are you okay?"

"I'm fine." She had a soft, even voice, and shiny beautiful black hair.

"This is Joel," Paul said. "My sister, Kiki."

"Hi, Joel," she said. I could see what he meant about her being young. It was more her manner, very formal and old-fashioned. You just couldn't imagine her making out with someone, let alone going all the way. That guy must've had quite a line.

"We'll wait with you till your girl friend is done," Paul said. "Is that all right?" he asked his sister.

"Sure." She sat down.

"It didn't hurt?" he said again with that same worried expression.

"No, not at all." She looked at me. "You don't have to worry about your girl friend. You hardly feel anything."

That made me feel guilty because actually I hadn't been worrying at all. And I felt guilty, too, because here was this really nice, pretty girl and just because her brother had told me she'd had sex, I was starting to think of her that way. I know that if everyone's thoughts were broadcast over a loudspeaker, we'd probably all be in big trouble, maybe even in jail, but I still felt bad, like I should only have been thinking of Leda.

While we waited, I played a game of chess with Kiki. She was terrific. She beat me in six moves. I'm not sure exactly what happened. It's possible I wasn't concentrating that hard. "I play a lot," she apologized.

"I used to."

I couldn't help wondering who her boyfriend was and how many times they'd done it and whether she'd thought she loved him. An image of her naked flashed through my mind while her brother was putting the chess set away. And here they were both being so nice, waiting for me!

"It's nice of you to come with your girl friend," she said when Paul had gone out a minute to the bathroom. "I know she appreciates it. If I hadn't had Paul . . ."

"Yeah, well, I wanted to."

"You love each other very much?"

The way she was looking at me with those soft black eyes, I had to say, "Yes."

"I'm glad," she said and kept staring at me. In some ways she was as pretty as Angelica's bridesmaid, but in a different way. Not as sexy, as far as her figure or her personality went, but her face was just as pretty.

When Leda came out about ten minutes later, she looked startled, seeing me talking with Kiki and Paul. "How'd it go?" I said.

"Fine," she said lightly. She sounded a little dreamy. "Who're you?" she said to Paul and Kiki.

I introduced them.

"Hey, let's all go out and celebrate," Leda said, to them as well as me. "Do you want to? I have this great grass. Do you want to come over to my house?"

I was sure they'd say no, but they said they'd like to. Leda hadn't mentioned anything about the grass to me before. When we were outside, she said, "It hurt."

"I'm sorry," I said.

"They said it wouldn't." She frowned. "Why do people lie about things?"

"They shouldn't," Paul said. "I'm going to be a doctor and I'll never lie."

"I know," Leda said intently. "I know you won't."

I don't know how she could know that when she'd only known him for five minutes! Leda is like that. She just starts talking to people as if she'd known them all her life.

We took a cab, the four of us, back to Leda's apartment. Her parents had left for the weekend so we had the place to ourselves. I'd told Mom and Dad I was staying at Berger's. Leda made spaghetti for us and we ate it in her room on the floor. Then we all got stoned. I was kind of amazed that Kiki and Paul wanted to. They both seemed so, not square, but very polite and slightly uptight. Leda really went off. Maybe it was just the tension of the whole thing and wanting to forget, but she began saying all kinds of personal things that sort of embarrassed me, even though I wasn't quite there either. She was lying on the floor with her head on a pillow. "Do you like sex?" she asked Paul. "I mean, do you think it's worth it?"

"I don't know," he said. "I never did it."

Leda looked at him. Her hair was falling into her face. "You mean, you're a virgin?"

He nodded.

"How come?" She passed the joint to Kiki.

Paul laughed. "No one ever asked me," he said.

"No one ever asked you!" Leda said, giggling. "Why?"

"I don't know. . . . I guess I'm not the type."

"No," Leda said firmly. "You're the type. Don't worry. I can tell. You'll love it. . . . But you have to wait for the right girl. That's important. Don't do it with just anyone."

"I won't," he promised her. He was staring at her in a slightly mesmerized way. It could have been the grass, but I wondered if he was falling in love with her. I was too woozy to figure it out. Kiki was just sitting there quietly.

"*I* waited," she said in that soft voice. "I loved him."

"He was a jerk," Paul said angrily.

"He wasn't!" Kiki said. "I *loved* him."

"She loved him," Leda said to Paul. "She wouldn't have loved him if he wasn't . . . something. You'll find out when it happens to you." She looked over at me. "Won't he?"

"What?" I said.

"He'll find out," she said. She closed her eyes. "Oh, I feel so . . . glad not to be pregnant. It's a wonderful feeling. No more baby."

"I love babies," Kiki said.

"I love other people's babies," Leda said. "Babies love me, or at least this one baby I sit for . . . I think he's kind of in love with me." She looked at Kiki. "Do you think they're in heaven now? Do you believe in God?"

"Who?" Kiki said.

"Our babies."

Kiki shook her head.

"I don't either," Leda said mournfully. Then she started to cry.

Paul went over and put his hand on her shoulder. "Don't feel bad," he said.

I felt jealous and angry that he'd done that before I'd even thought of it. I felt like I couldn't even move. I was so sleepy and out of it. I guess that grass was stronger than I thought.

Leda was sniffing a little while he kept patting her arm. "Someday you'll get married and have many babies," he promised her.

"Will I?" Leda said, like he was some kind of psychic who could see into the future.

"Yes," he said firmly.

"Will they be boys or girls?" Leda said, looking up at him.

"Which do you want?"

"One of each."

"That's what you'll get, then."

Leda lay there, staring off dreamily. "And you'll get a beautiful, wonderful girl who'll fall madly in love with you."

I looked at Kiki. I felt a little like we were two people at a slightly strange play. She smiled at me. "How about us?" she said a little ironically.

"You'll be fine too," Leda said. "We're all going to be fine."

At around midnight Kiki and Paul left. We all hugged and kissed each other good-bye. It was hard to believe we'd only met them a few hours earlier. After they left, we went back into Leda's room. The grass was starting to wear off a little.

"They were so nice!" Leda said.

"Yeah," I agreed. Then I couldn't help adding, "He seemed to really like you. I guess it was mutual."

Leda looked at me angrily. "Well, I wasn't the one who picked them up!" she said. "My back was turned, like, one *second* and you've picked up some cute little Oriental girl. If I'd been gone an hour, you could've had a whole harem!"

"I didn't pick her up," I explained. "I started talking to him and . . ."

Suddenly Leda hugged me. "Oh, it doesn't matter. Let's not fight, Joel! Please?"

"Sure," I said, keeping my arms around her. I knew we couldn't do anything for a few days, but I wanted the feeling of holding her close like that. It seemed like we'd been so far apart in every way the last few weeks. "I don't want to fight."

"Everything'll be different now," she said. "I'll go on the Pill. We can start over."

"Right," I said. "We'll start over."

We lay down together in her bed and, I guess because of the grass or just being worn out, we fell sound asleep with all our clothes on. When I woke up, it was Saturday morning and the sun was streaming in the window.

❦ 21 ❦

It wasn't the same, though, after that. Maybe you can't start over, I don't know. We still saw each other in the month or so till school ended and we made love a couple of times, but something was different. When I went off to Europe for the summer, it was like we both knew it was over, even though we had never had a major fight or "broken up" in any formal sense. Even now, four months later, I can't exactly figure out what happened. I've wondered a lot how much of it had to do with Leda's getting pregnant. If she hadn't, would we still be seeing each other? I don't know. I don't even know if we stopped being in love with each other, but it was never the same after that.

I won't go into a big thing about my summer except to say it was terrific. I spent most of the two months in Paris, though I took a few trips toward the end. Berger's uncle was great. He's part of this rock band over there and he let me help out at the club he plays in, sitting in on rehearsals and even playing with them sometimes. I guess the main thing I realized, spending most of the summer with guys whose profession is music, is that mine isn't going to be. It isn't just a matter of how good you are or how much you practice, though naturally that counts too. It was that these guys just cared about music in some kind of total way that I don't. I love it and I loved doing it and listening to them, but there was a difference. Berger's uncle said something like that to me once, I forget exactly how he put it. He said, "You're not possessed." Most of the time he talked to me in French, even though he's American. I guess after living there ten years French seems more natural to him.

My French got better too, but it seemed like even toward the end a lot of French people had trouble understanding what I was saying. I think it was my accent more than that I didn't know enough words or got the grammar wrong, though I wasn't always sure about my grammar. That may have been why not that much happened with me and girls. You'd think—what a perfect setup. Three months in Paris and all that. What can I say? I just didn't meet any of those dark-haired sexy types that Leda's father talked about. Or I'd meet them but they'd treat me like a real kid, just someone it was fun to talk to, but that's all. There was maybe one girl, maybe one and a half where anything might even have happened, but there I really did feel the language thing was a hindrance. Maybe for someone with a different personality it wouldn't have been. But if someone says "Pardon?" after everything you're saying, it's hard to feel relaxed *or* that sexy. So the long and short of it is there hasn't been anyone since Leda.

Even with Lassie nothing happened. There it may have been more that she was only in Paris for two days and she was just getting over the flu so she wasn't feeling that hot. I gather they really had done a lot of bicycling so she was kind of exhausted. We had a good time, though. I took her to a restaurant I knew and we talked till two in the morning. It may have been that we'd both built it up almost too much in our minds. We'd been writing back and forth all summer. So when we finally met again, it was a little bit of a letdown. We still plan to see each other. She's going to Wellesley, which isn't that far from Yale, so we may get together some weekend and, who knows, something might happen then.

Oh, yeah, I meant to mention that. I got into Yale. My parents called me in the middle of the summer. They sounded really excited, Dad especially. I'd kind of forgotten about even being on the waiting list. Anyway, I said I'd go. I figured just because Dad went there and Leda was going there wasn't enough of a reason to turn it down. At least it's close to New York.

So far I've been at college about six weeks. My classes are hard, more work than high school, but not impossible. I think I can make it. I called Leda the first week I got here and we arranged to meet for coffee. Somehow that seemed easier than going on a regular date. Then the afternoon it was set up, she called and said she was swamped with work and wondered if we could do it another time. She sounded friendly, so I didn't take it personally. The trouble was, the next time I was sick. Not so I had to go to the hospital, but I had a fever and a pretty lousy cold. "Well, listen, call me when you're feeling better," she said. I said I would, but by then it was, like, maybe we were both getting the idea that, even though we might be friends or whatever, the other part of our relationship was kind of finished. One day I passed her on campus, holding hands with some guy. We waved, but that was all. I felt pretty shitty the rest of the day.

Actually, there are a few really nice seeming girls in a few of my classes and one I know likes me, Phillipa Kranz.

She always sits next to me and we had coffee once after class. So don't worry about me. I don't feel like a social failure. I just don't feel like rushing into anything right away.

Around Halloween Berger, Ingrid, and Hopie came up to visit me for the weekend. Berger's going to Sarah Lawrence. He commutes from the city. He and Ingrid are living together. Figure that one out. If anyone should've broken up, it was him. But they really get along. At first his parents were a little hysterical about his living with "an older woman," his mother especially, but once they met Ingrid, they liked her a lot, and could see that she's had a "stabilizing influence" on Berger. It's true. His grades are ten times better than they were in high school. I think maybe Ingrid's helping him with his science courses.

Over the summer he did summer stock in Massachusetts and she came up to see him. He says it's perfect. By the time she's set up in her practice as a shrink, he'll be out of college and starting to try and make it as an actor in a serious way. So she can support him for the first ten years or so. I've stopped joking with him about it. He's definitely in love. For a long time I couldn't believe that, but if you see them together, you see that for some weird reason it works. It's impossible to understand why, but it does.

The week before they were going to come up, I saw this announcement in the college paper about a play, *Strange Bedfellows*, that Leda was going to be in. It's funny. I never saw Leda act; she wasn't acting her last year of high school. She went to a lot of plays and movies and sometimes afterward we'd talk about someone's performance or she'd criticize the way someone had acted, but it was like a part of her life that was off to one side somewhere. So I was curious. When the three of them arrived, I asked if they felt like going and they said yes. I wasn't sure we'd be able to get tickets at the last minute, but it turned out we could, if we didn't mind sitting toward the front to one side.

It was a strange play. I guess it was written a pretty long time ago. It was set during a time when women didn't even have the vote! I guess you'd call it a comedy since everything pretty much ended up okay. There was stuff they'd never do nowadays like a Chinese servant who talked in this funny accent and dropped his *r*'s. Leda was playing someone named Clarissa. It was a pretty big part, kind of a lead, except it was the kind of play where a lot of people had leads. She looked different. It wasn't just that she was wearing stage makeup. Actually, you couldn't tell she was that much except her cheeks were kind of bright pink, but they can get like that when she's excited. She wore her hair back the way women did in those days and she had on a long dress with a thing in the back that Ingrid said was a bustle.

"Imagine having to dress like that!" she said after the first intermission.

"I think Leda's good," Berger said. Like most people who act, he's more critical than me. "She seemed nervous in the beginning, but she's really good."

"Is that your girl friend, Joel?" Hopie asked me, tugging excitedly at my sleeve. "Is that her?"

I swallowed. "Well, she used to be."

"Isn't she anymore?"

"Not really."

"Is she in love with someone else? Is she in love with the man in the play?"

"Hopie, pipe down," Berger said. "He's a mess," he added. "Who is he?"

"I don't know," I said. "I think he's a senior."

In the play the idea was that Leda (Clarissa) had just gotten married to a guy named Matthew who was a congressman. You gathered he was supposed to be kind of a

209

stud, or at least a really handsome, charming guy that women fall for. She was a suffragette and that's what the plot was about. He didn't want her to be and she thought she could convince him to go over to her side and he thought he could convince her to go over to his side and they had a big fight about it.

"What don't you think was good about him?" I asked Berger. Even though it was just a play, I felt a little jealous when the guy started kissing Leda.

"He can't act, that's all," Berger said. "He's wooden."

"He's handsome, though," Hopie said. "Don't you think so?"

Ingrid sniffed. "That Greek god type is a bore," she said. She does have this very cool, definite way of saying things, as if there is only one opinion and that is it. Berger looked pleased. No one can accuse him of looking like a Greek god, that's for sure. Actually, he's looking pretty good. He lost some weight and he really stopped smoking. I guess he figured if he wanted to hang on to Ingrid, he'd better stay in some kind of shape.

In the last act there were two scenes that really got to me. First of all, I don't know if you've ever had this experience, but it's really strange seeing someone you've been in love with up on stage acting like they're in love with someone else. Even though it was over between us, to sit there and watch Leda flirting—which she's good at!—and blushing and having fights with someone who's supposed to be in love with her—well, it was painful, much more than I'd ever expected when I got the tickets.

In one scene she and her husband had a big fight. Not just verbal. He was trying to get her to sit still and at the same time shouting things like, "You're acting like an idiot." She was squirming around, shouting back, "I won't be coerced—just because you're stronger than I am." Then, at the end of the scene, she suddenly started crying and collapsed into his arms. Her voice got really low, like a purr. "I'm so terribly, so frighteningly in love with you," she said. "I've been betrayed by my emotions." At the end of the scene she made this speech, ending, "If all women are such a mass of unpredictable, uncontrollable emotions, they deserve to be classified with lunatics. We're not *fit* to vote." A lot of women in the audience booed, then a lot of people laughed, even though it wasn't supposed to be a funny scene.

Somehow what got to me was that, despite the old-fashioned language, Leda acted in that scene so much the way she used to in real life, getting all excited and angry, flirting, changing her mind and her mood so often you thought you were going crazy. I felt like I was up there, like I was the guy playing her husband. He just stood there staring at her in perplexity, like there must be some way to understand her but he didn't know what it was. In the end it worked out okay, like I said. He decided to back her in the suffragette thing and she forgave him for having tried to wreck some political campaign she was running. In the last scene he carried her off in his arms. She was laughing and cuddling against him, her face up against his chest. One woman yelled, "Boo!" but that was all.

Then it was over and they came out to take their bows. There was a lot of applause. I think the audience liked it, despite the booing. Leda got a big hand. She came out with the guy who played her husband, hand in hand, and they bowed together and then separately and smiled at each other.

The curtain came down. Hopie said, "Can we go backstage and get her autograph?"

Berger and Ingrid looked at me. I knew they were willing to do whatever I wanted. I wasn't sure. If Hopie hadn't suggested it, I never would have, but I said, "Sure, let's go."

211

There were a lot of people backstage, and it took awhile to find Leda's dressing room. It was a big one that she was sharing with a bunch of other girls. The door was open so we just walked in. She was standing, still in her old-fashioned dress, but with her hair loose and most of her makeup off. She still had on more eye makeup than she usually wears. "Oh, hi, Joel," she said, turning around. She saw me in the mirror first. "Hi, Berger."

I introduced Hopie and Ingrid. Hopie shoved the program at Leda. "Can I have your autograph?" she said.

"Sure," Leda said. She looked at me. "Do you have a pen?"

I didn't, but Ingrid did. Leda signed her name and gave it back to Hopie. "Are you up for the weekend?" she asked in a general way to Berger and Ingrid.

"Yeah," Berger said. "We thought we'd check it out, see if Joel was behaving himself. . . . You were good."

"Thanks." Leda laughed. "It's kind of a funny play, isn't it?"

"A little dated," Ingrid said.

"It's a good part," Leda said. "I never expected them to boo, though! That was funny."

"Did you mind?" Hopie asked.

"Well, it kind of breaks your mood, but I know what they mean. She does kind of collapse awfully easily."

"When you're in love, things get more complicated," Ingrid said, smiling. She and Berger were holding hands.

Leda glanced at me. "Yeah," she said softly. "True."

Just then this guy looked in. "You ready, Lee?" he said. It wasn't the guy who played her husband. It was the guy who played the teen-age brother.

"I'll be ready in about five minutes," Leda said. She introduced us to the guy, whose name was Ian.

"You looked different in the play," Hopie said.

He smiled down at her. Then he left, saying he'd be back

later. I wondered if he was Leda's new boyfriend. Hopie said she needed to go to the bathroom and Leda pointed out where it was. Ingrid said she'd go with her, and Berger kind of wandered off. I wasn't sure how I felt about that. I didn't know if I wanted to be alone with her.

"I got a letter from Paul," Leda said. "Remember him?"

"Sure."

"He might come up and visit. He says he and Kiki are thinking of applying here."

That seemed like such a long time ago, that night we all got stoned. "Do you like it, school, I mean?" Leda asked.

"Yeah, it's hard, though."

"I know! . . . I'm taking Greek. Wow, I hope I make it through the first semester."

"How come Greek?"

She shrugged. "I just thought it would be interesting." She looked at me a moment.

I hated myself for feeling so awkward with her. It was everything, her being in the costume, the fact that Berger and Ingrid might come back any minute. I was almost relieved when she said, "I guess I better change. They don't like us to stay around backstage too long."

Just as I was turning to go, she called out, "I'm glad you came."

"You were wonderful," I blurted out. I hadn't meant to say that. I turned red.

She smiled. "So, I'll see you around."

"Yeah." I was standing there in a daze when Berger and Ingrid came back with Hopie trailing behind them. "I guess we better go," I said. "She has to change."

"I'm going to get autographs of a lot of famous people," Hopie said, "and save them in an album."

Berger said, "Want mine, Hopie? *I'm* going to be famous."

She looked at him scornfully. "You don't count," she said.

Berger looked mock heartbroken. "I don't count? Oh, I can't take it. . . . I don't count!"

We made our way out of the theater. I looked back, wondering if Leda might come out, but she didn't. As we were walking to the car, we passed a movie theater. *Endless Love* was playing. Hopie got all excited. "I really want to see that," she said. "I heard it's terrific."

"You can't," Berger said. "You're too young. It's too dirty."

"I am *not* too young," Hopie said. "All my friends've seen it." She turned to me. "Will you take me, Joel?"

I hesitated. "I saw it already."

"Oh."

Maybe something in my voice was a giveaway, but when I turned Hopie was looking at me. Sometimes I think little kids understand a lot, more than grown-ups, even. She didn't say anything, but she took my hand and held it. It wasn't a romantic gesture, it was just a nice, terrific thing to have someone do at that particular moment.

Berger asked if we wanted to go somewhere to eat.

Young people learning to cope with the feelings and contradictions of growing up...

JUNIPER BOOKS

TAF-12